MW01244600

June Bride

A Year in Paradise #6

Hildred Billings
BARACHOU PRESS

June Bride

Copyright: Hildred Billings
Published: 10th June 2019
Publisher: Barachou Press

This is a work of fiction. Any and all similarities to any characters, settings, or situations are purely coincidental.

All rights reserved. No part of this publication may be reproduced, stored in retrieval system, copied in any form or by any means, electronic, mechanical, photocopying, recording or otherwise transmitted without written permission from the publisher. You must not circulate this book in any format.

Chapter 1

BRANDELYN

The one thing Dr. Brandelyn Meyer guaranteed her patients was undivided attention. Whether they came in with a small tingle in their tummy, or blood gushing from one of their orifices, the only full-time GP in Paradise Valley pulled up her stool and gave everything she had until the matter was resolved.

Or so she claimed until one month before her wedding.

Should I spring for those last-minute lessons? Her dog Brutus was easily trainable. He could learn how to carry a pillow of rings down the aisle. Ooh, wouldn't it be *adorable?* Her little Pomeranian was one of the most well-loved dogs in Paradise Valley. Brandy couldn't take him for a walk between Florida and Arizona Streets without the neighbors popping out to say hello and offer him treats. Wouldn't they absolutely lose it to see him in the wedding procession? Who was carrying the rings right now? Some second cousin she enlisted because he was the only boy under the age of eight in her family? *The things I do for tradition...*

"Doctor?"

Caught with her eyes glazed over, Brandelyn jerked upright on her stool and almost knocked her stethoscope off her shoulders. The clinging and clanging as she struggled to pull herself together made her patient jump, hand over heart.

"My apologies." Brandelyn cleared her throat and pushed her bangs out of her eyes. She always wore her long brown hair back, either in a low ponytail or a high bun that stayed out of the way. *For my wedding, I'll finally get to wear it down!* She had been looking forward to debuting her gorgeous long locks ever since she realized she could wear it however she wanted on her wedding day. With half of the town invited, that would be a *lot* of gasps. "I suddenly remembered something important that I have to do today. I shouldn't have been doing that, though. Now, what was it that you needed?"

Her patient, a thirty-something woman named Joan, folded her hands in her lap while her eyes darted back and forth in her skull. Brandelyn knew enough about nervous tics to detect her patient's lack of faith. *Great. Well, at least I have a captive audience in this town.* She was the only doctor for thirty miles in either direction and the first line of defense before referrals to the bigger towns and cities flew from her notepad. Most of what she saw were the usual non-emergency illnesses and injuries. Sometimes the appointment was mere formality to renew a prescription. Only once in the past year had she looked at a patient and told them to get the hell to the emergency room twenty-five miles away. Mr. Raymond Green wasn't going to last long with that heart attack thundering through him. (And, according to his last appointment a week ago, he was doing much better.)

"Our insurance changed this month," Joan reminded her doctor. She clutched her stomach and pointed her chin downward, as if the answers to her plight were in her lap. "Which means I need a referral to my usual OB/GYN. I gotta do it as soon as possible, obviously."

"Yes." Brandelyn looked at the test results on Joan's chart. "Well, far be it from me to keep you from getting the expert level of care you need." She said that with a genial smile. She had tone misconstrued before, and she would be damned if yet another patient took her demeanor to mean she was offended. "I'll have you talk to the receptionist. She'll take care of everything." A few signatures later, Joan had her precious referral to a specialist on the coast.

"Thank you so much! I wanted to come in early this month because I know you'll be busy later."

Finally! A reason to genuinely grin! "I'll be taking a couple of weeks off, all right. One week for the honeymoon, and one week to get some affairs sorted." She couldn't leave the paperwork up to her fiancée. Sunny was a well-meaning woman, but she was more caught up in her business than the doctor was in hers. Then again, outside of extreme emergencies, Brandy had much more constrained working hours. Sunny ran a bed and breakfast that saw a huge uptick in business during the summer months. Brandelyn wasn't looking forward to moving furniture and housewares around by herself. Let alone the day after getting back from her honeymoon... which she had planned down to the last minute. At least the deposits were made and the payments on her credit cards handled. Now, as for some of the wedding stuff... Brandy must remember to call her wedding planner about her ideas for the ring bearer.

"It sounds so fantastical," Joan said with a grin. "I always wanted to have a nice little wedding, but Lorri was very adamant she couldn't stand much more than City Hall and a nice dinner with friends. Then again, I say we 'only' have a domestic partnership right now. There's still room to register a proper marriage, yes?"

"From my understanding, absolutely." Sunny had come around to the idea of full-blown, nationally-recognized marriage, but it took convincing. At first, she wanted to get a domestic partnership. *"For tax reasons,"* she had said. That made Brandy drag her fiancée to the tax preparer's office for a small lesson in tax brackets and how they could totally get married without paying much more in federal taxes. Hesper Chess had looked like they touched down from another planet, but Brandy left no stone unturned on her path to the perfect wedding. *You can't have a wedding for* just *a domestic partnership...* Once she and Sunny decided to make their long-term relationship official, a wedding was the only thing Brandy cared about. Sunny knew this. She also knew that her fiancée had been planning the perfect wedding since she was four-years-old.

Brandelyn personally showed Joan back to reception. Once she ensured everything was taken care of, Brandy escaped to her office, where she shut the door and sank into her plush leather chair. Her next appointment block was free. Plenty of time to call the wedding planner!

She should have called Sunny first, but one of the most blessed things about planning a wedding with her? She didn't care nearly as much as Brandy, who lived and breathed wedding planning. Hell, sometimes she joked that she had been waiting her whole life to get married!

It started when Charles and Diana got married, hadn't it? Four-year-old Brandelyn, future doctor and core member of her small community, parked her butt in front of her father's Manhattan TV and beheld the royal spectacle that shook the world. Not until their son William got married a few years ago had Brandy seen anything else like it. *You bet your ass I took the day off to watch that!* She was also stealing plenty of glances at her phone the day that actress from "Suits" married Harry. Nobody really understood her fascination with ostentatious weddings. Especially not in Paradise Valley, where humble mentalities met complete eschewing of heterosexual practices. While it wasn't uncommon to see lesbian couples in tux and dress – or two dresses, no less – there was nothing about it that screamed they did it because they simply had to. Brandy accepted that she was an outlier. Part of the reason she moved west after growing up in New York was to expand her horizons – and to find the kind of woman who jived with her best. *A simple country girl. Simple in practice and desires.* She had found that woman in Sunny Croker, a homegrown Paradise Valley gal who didn't look a day over thirty when they met seven years ago. It took two more years for them to start going out – Brandy had been much too busy taking over the only practice in town to properly date, but she always had her eye on the lovely lady in plaid and jeans who made weekly appearances at the library, bank, supermarket, and lesbian bar. The whole reason Brandy went to that dive every Friday night was for a chance to see Sunny!

How nobody snatched her up before me, I have no idea. Sunny claimed she hadn't dated much. Yet she was a total pro in the sack. *Uh huh. Didn't date much.* Maybe not seriously dated...

Brandy kept her giggles to herself as she plucked her phone off her desk. One year ago, she asked Sunny to marry her, setting in motion the events that led to this month.

I'm finally getting married. I'm finally getting the wedding of my dreams.

The little four-year-old watching royal weddings on TV had no idea what would finally happen forty years later. Her, in a wedding dress to make Kate Middleton *cry*. Her gorgeous fiancée, the sweetest woman in paradise valley, in a fitted tuxedo that turned the usual groom's cake topper on his head!

The aesthetics were perfect. Well, almost.

"Hello, Debbie? Great! It's me, Brandy!" As if Debbie would ever forget Brandelyn, the woman who blew up her phone every damn day. "Listen, I had the *cutest* idea for the wedding. How hard do you think it would be to strap the ring pillow to Brutus and train him to walk down the aisle by himself? People would go crazy, right? Oh, he's totally fine with a crowd. This is the boy who jumps through hoops every Fourth of July at the dog parade."

Debbie gave her a less than enthusiastic response. It was enough!

Chapter 2

SUNNY

"You really must try this one." Sunny climbed down her stool, but did not bother to shut the pantry doors. Her guest, the only one in the house at the time, sat at the large farmhouse table by the big paned windows overlooking the immaculately groomed acreage that made up Waterlily House. (However, there were no waterlilies to be seen on the property, outside of a few paintings and other motifs Sunny added through the years.) "You can buy these at the farmer's market, but I get them wholesale directly from the supplier. Go on. Try the marionberry one and tell me it doesn't melt on your tongue."

Fleur Rosé, a hotshot actress who recently instigated a media storm when she was caught dating a local from Paradise Valley, tittered to receive the sampling of jam. Four others already lined up before her plate of pancakes and toast. Fleur lamented that she really shouldn't be loading up on carbs before resuming the filming of some mini-series, but how could she *refuse* when she was a glutton for homemade jams and jellies?

Good thing Sunny had plenty to go around. The wares from a local farm were all the rage with her guests. Once she saw that most of the five-star reviews mentioned "the delicious local foods on hand," she knew she had to step up her game to keep people coming back every year while referring their friends to her when they were in the area. The B&B industry wasn't as booming in the days of people renting out their homes, but Sunny Croker knew how to combine her love of countryside hospitality with small town individuality. People who came to Paradise Valley wanted a proper experience. They loved the kitschy décor and the well-maintained grounds that allowed them to go hiking, partake in some light gardening, or use the scenery as inspiration for their next artistic endeavor. The amount of painters and writers who came to stay a few days rivaled the tourists and extended families who needed extra bedrooms to use. It helped that Waterlily House was only a mile out of town, but looked like it was completely isolated in the Oregonian woods. Most people borrowed bikes from the garage for their excursions into town.

Fleur was one of many who enjoyed the isolative aspect while appreciating the easy access. As a celebrity, she needed a certain layer of security, hence her careful planning of when to come. If Sunny said nobody else was due to be a guest – although she couldn't assure there would be no last-minute additions… without a fee, anyway – then that was fine with Fleur, who helped herself to the biggest guest room. Sunny often cooked breakfast for her guests, but admitted she liked it when there was only one, and that one really loved her jams and jellies.

"Oh, it's *divine!*" Fleur's eyes fluttered shut as she groaned onto the piece of toast in her mouth. Sunny held back a laugh. *She's gotta be kidding me.* Fleur was sweet, but she definitely played up the Hollywood angle a little too well. "I've had more than a few marionberry-flavored things over the years, but this is absolutely heavenly. What brand is it again?" She swallowed and picked up the jar from the table. "I love it. I wish I could be around for the farmer's market. I'll have to send Jalen to pick some up for me."

"I can call the farm and ask them to hold some. What flavors do you want?"

"You know them?"

"Oh, hon," Sunny said with a chuckle. "It's a small town and I run a hospitality business. I know everyone around here, whether they know it or not."

Their laughter was only interrupted by Sunny's phone ringing on the kitchen table. She excused herself to answer, which worked in

Fleur's favor. She was more than happy to chow down on jam-covered toast.

The smile on Sunny's face fell when she saw the name of a certain wedding planner. "Hello?" she said, attempting to keep the serenity on her face. "What's going on now?"

Debbie blew a breath laced in awkward chuckles. "So I'm guessing you haven't heard what your fiancée is planning now?"

"Do I want to know?" Sunny leaned against the counter.

"It involves firing the current ring bearer and replacing him with *Brutus*."

"Oh my Goooood." Sunny's eyes rolled far back into her head. Brutus was an adorable dog that made the animal lover inside of her leap for joy, but Brandy's cousin would be heartbroken if her son was booted from the wedding party at the last moment. For a dog, no less. "Let me guess. She saw something on Facebook and decided we're not really married unless we do that too?"

"She says it will make Brutus feel like a part of the family."

"He's a dog." Sunny had great respect for man's furry friends, but she had a feeling that Brutus didn't give his stubby tail whether or not he was "really family." The boy got walked, fed, and belly-rubbed. He might as well have been a kid trapped in Disneyland.

"I give it a day or two before she loses interest," Debbie said. "You know her better than I do. Maybe remind her that her this is her favorite cousin she might be offending."

Sunny couldn't help but laugh again. "You're right, I *do* know her better than you do." Once Brandy married a certain idea, she never divorced it. She was happily polyamorous with her ideas, such as telling Sunny she should continue to live at Waterlily House while simultaneously taking up permanent residence in Brandy's on Florida Street. Which made it all the more frustrating when she changed plans at the last minute.

"Well, consider this your warning. She might conveniently forget to tell you."

"Of course. Not like I'm supposed to help plan this shindig or anything."

"Trust me, if you were my primary contact for your wedding, I'd be on Cloud Nine."

"Just don't tell me how much she's paying you to put up with her bull." Brandy had money to burn, but not *that* much. Sunny always knew thousands of dollars would fall into the pit that was this wedding. She simply hoped it wouldn't be *tens* of thousands. Brandy's dress alone reportedly cost five.

Debbie happily continued at the reminder she was getting paid for her troubles. "While I have you on the phone, here's a friendly reminder that you have your tux fitting in Beaverton on the tenth. If you're the type to binge eat before big events, I suggest you do so before the fitting. Things will be much more comfortable on the wedding day."

"Only four more weeks, right?" They were getting married on the thirtieth. Practically Fourth of July weekend, which might actually work in their favor if they wanted most of their invited guests to attend. *Three hundred people. I can't imagine it. We know three hundred people?* "Then twe can go back to normal."

"Nothing's the way it used to be after you get married, dear."

That was Sunny's cue to hang up.

"I think I like the strawberry and marionberry ones the most. Maybe blueberry for Jalen." Fleur caught Sunny's attention by stacking three jam jars on top of each other. They looked the delightful, colorful sight on their perch. "Everything okay with the phone?"

Were they so close now that she had no qualms asking such personal questions? Then again, Sunny was used to it. The city-folk – never mind out of touch celebrities – who came to her humble house loved to pry, like Sunny was some bumpkin of a specimen.

"That was my wedding planner informing me that my fiancée is getting crazy ideas again."

"Ooh, you're getting married? Congratulations!"

"Thank you. Happening at the end of the month." Couldn't come too soon. As excited as Sunny was to marry her fiancée, she couldn't say this whole wedding debacle gave her the same joy. *This is all Brandy's thing...* She had known it would be from the moment Brandelyn popped the question. This was the woman who owned stacks of old bridal magazines and watched every wedding show on TV. She would peruse bridal shops on her days off, *long* before any engagement was on the table. Sunny knew this. She accepted it. Brandelyn was a traditional romantic who got off on the event as much as the person she shared it with – she must have known that Sunny was *the one* because she never once said anything about it.

Everyone had their thing, after all. If the worst Brandelyn got was when she planned her first wedding, then that wouldn't be so bad. *She'll be planning every anniversary party until we die.* This would still be the worst, and it would soon be out of the way.

"I had heard there was a big wedding happening in town this month," Fleur said. "I had no idea it was yours."

"I don't know about that. There are always a few every summer. Mostly tourists." No, it was hers. Nobody else was a local inviting over three hundred people. "We'll be having the wedding here, so the B&B will be closed for a week while we get things ready and house some of our extended family." Brandelyn's mother and sister's family would be staying with her at the house on Florida Street. Sunny didn't have as much family coming to stay at Waterlily House, but she had plenty of room for some of Brandy's cousins... and her father, making his first grand appearance from Manhattan in God knew how many years. "She originally wanted to have the wedding at the 'cutest church in town,' but we aren't members, and that would've been a little weird." Luckily, Brandy's mood was saved when Sunny suggested they get married at Waterlily House. The views were to die for, and the weather was usually amicable every late June. *The only reason she wants to get married in a church is because that's what she's always imagined.* Brandelyn was far from religious – for shit's sake, her relations were Jewish! – so it had nothing to do with the sanctity of marriage or presenting it before God. She wanted the picture-perfect imagery that would go down in Paradise Valley history as *unforgettable.*

"Do you have your dress picked out?" Fleur's girlish giggles lulled Sunny out of her complicated thoughts. "That's always my favorite part. Seeing what the bride is wearing!" She paused. "Or is that the brides in this case?"

"I'm wearing a tux," Sunny said.

"Ooooh. You'll be quite dashing! You really have the face for it."

Sunny snorted. "Thanks, I guess."

"Trust me, I've seen a lot of tuxes in my day. The people who pull them off the most are those with confident jawlines. You can have tits for days and hair down to your ass, but if you have that jaw? You're the most dapper person in the room."

Sunny honestly had no idea what to say. *No one has ever commented on my jaw before.* She was suddenly self-conscious. What if her round face lost its neck on the big day? She'd be drowning in a full tux while Brandy, who was already two inches taller than her fiancée, traipsed down the aisle in her giant princess gown. *Not that I know what her dress looks like. She won't let me see it.* The more Sunny thought about what a "traditionalist" her queer fiancée was, the more she either wanted to laugh or sigh. At least it meant Brandy would probably wear a garter, and that would be good fun on the wedding night. *That's the part I'm looking forward to the most...* They hadn't had sex in over a month, thanks to busy lives and the stress of planning a wedding up to the last moment. Brandy may have been doing the bulk of the planning, but Sunny wasn't immune to the stress.

She had a secret, though. In the midst of the planning and wishing that things would be over soon, Sunny had been participating in some major treats of her own. One currently hung in the back of her closet. Far, far back, in case Brandelyn happened to stumble in there without minding her own business.

When we first got engaged, I imagined something completely different. She knew Brandy would have the most gorgeous bridal gown in Paradise Valley, but Sunny had no idea she would be wearing a tux until her fiancée helpfully informed her around Christmas. By then, Sunny had already bought a dress of her own. A simple off-the-shoulder gown that showed off her best feature, her clavicle. The seamstress who took in the dress she got off a sale rack told Sunny that she looked like a "lovely country princess" with her short, blond hair and big smile. *I sure did smile a lot when I tried it on after the seamstress was done taking it in.* It was going to be a surprise to Brandelyn for their fifth anniversary that past December. Instead, she discovered she was going to wear a tux, because *of course* she was.

I should have said something. Yet for some inexplicable reason, she didn't say a damn thing when Brandy looked at her as if it would be her greatest dream come true to marry someone in a tuxedo. How could Sunny say no to that? It wasn't like she spent a lot of money on her own dress. Not nearly as much as Brandelyn, who went to a boutique in Portland and tried on everything until she reportedly "cried her eyes out" to finally discover the perfect dress.

If Sunny had one major fault, it was her inability to say no to people she loved. Before, it had landed her in the kinds of waters that were obnoxious at worst, relatively harmless at best. But now, as she came upon the eve of her wedding, she realized more and more that she had made such concessions that might have put her own tastes in jeopardy.

The knot in her chest every time she thought about the wedding wasn't from the cold feet of getting married and connecting herself to one person for the rest of her life. It was the thought of being the center of attention of a spectacle she had nothing to do with. Not outside of Brandy's grand "vision," anyway.

Chapter 3

BRANDELYN

The turkey burgers sizzled in the pan while the home fries baked in the oven. Brandelyn nibbled on a cherry tomato as she dithered between the frying pan and the salad she tossed in a large bowl made of local myrtle wood. So was the spoon doing most of the tossing. There was something about the smooth texture of myrtle wood, wasn't there? Even when drenched in dressing, Brandy took great pleasure in running her fingers over the fine wood that cost her a pretty penny to have in the house.

So did the turkey burgers, since God knew the supermarket gouged everyone for *beef,* let alone turkey. Brandy bought most of her meat in the city and froze it for later. Occasionally, a grateful hunter gave her hunks of deer meat in thanks for treating somebody in the family, but it had been a while since she last had any in her stores. The turkey had been supposedly on sale, and Dr. Meyer was the first one to tell anyone how much better turkey meat was for the body. If they had to eat meat, anyway... but like most people who didn't practice what they preached, Brandelyn had yet to transfer to vegetarianism.

Although these sweet cherry tomatoes from her garden made a compelling argument!

She picked up the remote from the counter and turned down the stereo playing her old and worn Shania Twain CD. Just in time, too, for the back door only a few feet away swung open and admitted her favorite person.

"Hey." Sunny dumped a plastic bag full of freshly harvested potatoes onto the counter. "Surprise. The first earlies from the garden are ready. Thought we might like some soon."

"Excellent. That will replace what I threw in the oven." Brandy dropped her spoon, stepped away from the stove, and offered her fiancée a kiss on the cheek. *She has the best cheeks for kissing.* Brandelyn still got excited to see those puffy cheeks with the most elastic skin in Paradise Valley. The whole reason she crushed on Sunny, back before she knew about the affinity for all things wholesome and simple, was because of those kissable cheeks. *First time I saw her was the library. I thought, "Who is that beautiful woman in short hair and flannel?" Which is a big thing to think in a town like this...* Short hair and flannel was one of the acceptable uniforms about town. Sunny wore it well, although she was shorter and a bit more filled out than some of the other butches in Paradise Valley. So happened the "soft butch" look appealed to Brandy. The first time she saw Sunny in a summery sundress made their date to the beach one to remember.

"Yo, Earth to Dr. Meyer." Sunny snapped her fingers around her fiancée's faraway gaze. "Your burgers are burning."

Brandy squealed to hear the grease spitting like it had nothing else to do. She turned down the stove and moved the pan to another burner.

She and Sunny hadn't as many chances to eat together over the past few weeks. The busy season at Waterlily House had begun, and when Sunny wasn't entertaining her guests, she was busy in the garden or running errands all over town. Didn't help that Brandelyn had her own schedule to adhere to most of the week. Some doctors took four days off a week, but not Dr. Meyer. She only got *three* at the most. She loved her three-day weekends that included a robust Monday full of sleeping in and lazing about in front of the TV.

Of course, it was better if she could spend her time with Sunny. That's why a stolen night together like that one was priceless.

Besides! They had much to talk about.

"Candles? Really? What anniversary have I forgotten?" Sunny's hand lingered on Brandy's as she leaned in to light the tealights spaced out on her dining table. *My God, look at that face in candlelight.* Brandelyn had turned off the lights to allow nothing but the candlelight to illuminate the room. Shadows stripped the trees in her backyard, but her south-facing window meant it stayed relatively bright well until sundown. A total boon in the winter. *Why I have no intention of selling and moving to Waterlily House.* It was close enough to town to be a fine commute to the clinic, but Brandy couldn't stand the thought of having strangers in her house at any moment. Right now, Sunny lived in the mother-in-law suite at Waterlily House, a property she inherited from her aunt ten years ago. Brandelyn was the one enticing her partner to come live with her in town, yet Sunny claimed it wasn't good business to stay too far away from the guesthouse. *At least live with me during the slower months...* She had a lot of repeat customers in the likes of professionals getting away for a few days and artists looking for inspiration. They didn't need her around all the time, surely. Only during the crazier summer festivals...

...Which kept Brandelyn perfectly busy as well, so it worked out!

"I don't believe it's any of our anniversaries," although Brandy was absolutely the one in the relationship who would keep track of such things, "but I thought it would be lovely to have a little romance. Things are only going to get crazier as the wedding gets closer. Who knows when we'll have a chance like this again? And on such a lovely day."

Sunny glanced out the window. That close to the 45th parallel, and with DST in full effect, the evenings in their neck of the woods lasted as long as 8:30 or 9:00 PM. Their plans for a late afternoon wedding and evening reception was perfect for that time of year. As long as the weather cooperated, they looked forward to picturesque lighting and cooler temperatures as the sun set behind a canopy of old growth.

"It was nice today, wasn't it?" Sunny said, her smile as beautiful as her name. She helped herself to the salad in its wooden bowl. "Slow day at the house, too. I only have one guest right now, and she mostly keeps to herself."

Brandy struggled to remember who was at Waterlily House. "Is it that actress?"

"Yes, but you shouldn't go around telling people that. I had enough problems as it was with her security going over my whole property looking for cameras. I kept telling them we only have a doorbell camera, really, but I guess those Hollywood types deal with a lot of weird crap. She seems nice enough, though. Sold some Wolf's Hill Jam to her, so, guess you could say she's driving sales around here."

"You know, some of my patients have been murmuring about out-of-towners popping up and taking pictures before hopping back into their cars." Brandelyn poked at her food, but the intrigue of what she was about to say was too juicy to ignore. "Heaven said lots of people with big pro cameras keep coming into her café. Some of them snapped pictures. They won't tell her what's going on, though. Everyone has this conspiracy that the mayor is involved. You ask me, it's developers. That Portland gentrification sprawl will come for us sooner rather than layer."

Sunny chuckled. "We're a bit too far away from Portland for that to happen."

"You say that now, but you weren't there when it started." Brandelyn was an alumni of Oregon Health & Science University, and survived her residency at one of the Portland metros many hospitals. Those were the days of the gritty, grimy city starting to see developments along the South Waterfront and in the Pearl, a place that has previously held a not-so-shiny reputation. *You look at it today and barely recognize it.* Brandy had fond memories of stumbling drunk through downtown with her friends. Back then, "Keep Portland Weird" meant guys in tie-dye shirts offering guru advice for the payment of "one of your socks." Today, it meant that same guy strung out on meth threatening to put people in the hospital for crossing his path.

Real shame. Brandelyn thanked her lucky stars she saw opportunity in a place like Paradise Valley. It was close enough to the metro that they could take care of business when necessary, but far enough away that most of the mess didn't quite touch Paradise. Yet Brandy wasn't naïve. As people continued to be priced out of Portland and moved to its outskirts, those goal posts would continue to move until Paradise Valley was incorporated into the continuous sprawl. They were in the mountains, halfway between the Willamette Valley and the coast, but she could see it happening in her lifetime. *Assuming we don't go under with the big earthquake.*

"Are you thinking about the earthquake again?" Sunny asked. "You always get that look on your face when you're thinking about dying to the elements."

"I didn't know I had a face specifically for *that*."

"I've known you long enough that I can see it. You get the same face every time we go to the beach and you start fantasizing about tsunamis."

"Fantasizing? Is that what it is?"

"I know you like to swim, Brandy, but that really isn't the way..."

It took Brandelyn a moment to realize her fiancée was joking. One nudge of the arm later, they were back to eating their dinners while

Brutus the Pomeranian trotted into the kitchen to beg for a snack.

"No," Brandy curtly said, albeit in her cutesy puppy voice. "You've already had your dinner, Brutie."

Sunny ripped off a piece of her turkey burger and tossed it beneath the table. Brutus instantly went to her, little tail wagging so happily that he was compelled to bark before snarfing up the meat.

"Don't do that!" Brandelyn scolded her fiancée. "You're instilling bad manners!"

"Lighten up, hon. It's not like he's a real kid you can reason with. He's a dog. Let him live a little."

"Says the woman who..."

"Grew up on a farm?" Sunny's droll voice was accompanied with an eyeroll. "Let animals have some fun. I'm not gonna give him my whole burger."

That's not what Brutus assumed, though. He plopped down on his butt and stared hopefully at Sunny, tongue hanging out the side of his mouth. *See? He thinks he's getting more. Now he's going to keep doing this every time there's a whiff of meat at the table.* Brandy was grateful she and Sunny had decided on no kids, although they were not opposed to hosting the teenagers from their extended families for summers and breaks. Sunny's younger cousins were interested in helping out at the B&B over summers, and Brandelyn had a few nieces and nephews who could stand to get out of New York and have some real fresh air. (That was her expert, doctorly opinion, by the way.) But Brandy didn't have the patience for small children, and Sunny was such a quiet introvert that her fiancée couldn't imagine the smallest brood of kids running around underfoot. *Thank God menopause is coming up.* According to Brandelyn's family history, she had three years at most to enjoy menopause-free life. She already had gray hairs and crow's feet. Sunny, with her youthful glow, must have found them attractive, though. *She looks younger than I did at her age.* Sunny was thirty-seven, but most people took her for twenty-five at the oldest. Maybe thirty if she were tired.

"By the way," Brandy said, ignoring her begging fur-child. "Did you get that appointment set up with the tailor in Hillsboro? You know this is the busiest time of year for them, and..."

Sunny cut her off. "Yes, I did. I have an appointment next week for my final fitting."

She said it so stoically that Brandelyn couldn't help but cock her head, half-eaten turkey burger hovering in her hands. "If you're worried about the cost, Sun, you know I can..."

"It's fine." Sunny sniffed, eyes downcast to her plate. "Everything's fine. You know I hate driving to the metro, though."

Hillsboro barely counts. It was so far away that she had considered it a non-entity before she left Portland. Now she knew so many friends who had moved there as it developed more and more that it was like a different place.

"Well... I have my final wedding dress fitting next week, too." Brandy took her fiancée's hand and gave it a tight, affectionate squeeze. "I can't wait to show it to you. You're gonna adore it, Sun. The photographer will simply melt, too!"

A smile returned to Sunny's face. "I'm sure I will, hon. You always look beautiful when you dress up. Hell, you look like a million dollars right now."

It was a throwaway comment, yet Brandy blushed and tittered into her burger. *She's the first person to ever make me feel special.* Others had made her feel smart, even beautiful. She had been complimented from there to Timbuktu over the years, but Sunny was the first to look into her eyes and like what she saw. Brandy had spent her whole life waiting for the perfect woman to come along who would bring that love and serenity to her existence. After a life of go, go, *go,* Brandelyn was more than ready to settle down.

"I can't wait to get married." With hands covered in grease, Brandy took her fiancée's and let out a sigh of happiness. "As excited as I am for the big event, I'm more excited to simply settle into our new lives together. I can't wait to spend the rest of my life with you, Sun."

Sunny's shoulders relaxed. Wonderful. She really shouldn't tense them up like that. As a doctor, Brandy feared for her partner's body. As a woman in love? She feared that there might be an underlying issue that somehow made her responsible.

When Sunny looked at her like that, though, with her little smile and a glint in her eyes, Brandy's fears melted away.

Chapter 4

SUNNY

"They better not mess with my dahlias." Sighing, Sunny sat back and wiped her brow. A small shovel, a watering can, and a flat of impatiens ready for transfer lay beside her. *Lord, am I talking to the air again?* She could have sworn there was another soul only a few steps behind her, but she couldn't see them now.

Five seconds later, her close friend Anita Tichenor stepped forward, gardening gloves gracing her hands. "Why would anybody mess with your dahlias?" she asked. "You have the best dahlias in the county. They'd have to have a death wish once the locals heard about it."

"Nobody in Portland gives a crap about what the locals *here* think." Sunny took a swig of water from her canteen. Why did it have to be so warm? She dragged out her sunhat for this excursion to the grounds surrounding Waterlily House. English teacher Anita finally had some time to come help now that the school year was finished. *I am still not going to high school graduation, though.* Yeah, right. Sunny didn't know any of the students graduating that year. Not even Leigh Ann, the girl who sometimes helped out at the house during the summer. She did it for the mandatory volunteer credits, but seemed to genuinely enjoy the hospitality work. Not that she was here now. Leigh Ann was off on a family vacation, and honestly, Sunny couldn't stand the thought of a kid underfoot while she planned her wedding.

"Right," Anita said with a chuckle. "Your fiancée insisted on hiring that pro planner from Beaverton. Now we must all suffer as big city living comes to Paradise Valley."

Grumbles heaved from Sunny's chest as she recalled what Debbie the wedding planner said when she first heard Waterlily House would be the site of the ceremony and reception. "*Oh my Gooooooddd, we'll put the arch over here and the five tents for your three hundred guests over there! We'll only have to trim those bushes back a bit...*" Like hell they were coming for the rhododendron bushes Sunny's aunt planted forty years ago!

"Nobody's touching my dahlias," Sunny continued, grabbing the flat next to her, "and nobody's touching my impatiens." The whole reason she went down to the gardening shop to pick up pink and white impatiens was to contribute to the "aesthetic" of the ceremony, which would be held right here. Within two more weeks, this lovely, green, *empty* yard would be filled with chairs, arches, and pink bows. It was Sunny's idea to plant some flowers that matched the colors of their wedding, since she was planning on planting some new ones for the house, anyway, but boy did she regret mentioning it to Brandy and Debbie!

"When the big day comes and you're drowning in stress, I'll be sure to personally guard your flowers." Anita grabbed the shovel. "Hand me one of those flats, would you? We should get this done in time to enjoy some iced tea before I have to leave."

Sunny would be beyond lost without her friend. She and Anita had been close since the teacher returned to town to accept a position as Clark High School, although they knew each other as far back as enjoying student life at the same place. Anita was a year older than Sunny, but they still shared many lovely memories from their years as schoolgirls. *Class of 2000, represent.* Back then, it had been *beyond* cool to be the first class of the millennium. Too bad Sunny couldn't remember if that was her class or Anita's.

Anita was the one who kept her grounded while dating Brandy and finally accepting a marriage proposal. *She's the one with more experience than me, anyway.* Anita had never been married, but she lived with her partner of twelve years and had plenty of other experience before that. Whenever Sunny thought she felt crazy or needed a break from Brandy's neuroses, she ran to Anita. Likewise, Anita was usually around in the school teaching offseason to hang out on warm summer nights or help out around the house. Sunny was the only one on payroll, so she took all the help she could get.

Her friend was also her maid of honor. Brandelyn had asked her sister – the one she barely got along with, no less – and Anita often commented that the wedding was going to be its own special mess. *"This is why Bonnie and I have never gotten married, honestly,"* she had said more than once. *"Too much pressure for something we don't really care about."* Anita and her partner would probably get a courthouse marriage and never bother to tell anyone. If they hadn't already. If they ever did.

The iced tea was a welcomed refreshment after hours of digging around in the sun. Sunny always kept a pitcher of sun tea for her guests to consume, but since she didn't have any right now, she had free rein to add as many lemon slices as she and Anita liked. A sprinkle of sugar complemented the strong flavors as they sat in rocking chairs on the back porch. Neighboring hills rolled before them, a tranquil sight even in the middle of a dark, rainy winter.

When my aunt ran this place, it was my sanctuary. Sunny always struggled to make friends, let alone keep them, and it was worst when she was an awkward, sheltered child. Her mother had been Born Again and so wrapped up in her church life that Sunny often spent whole evenings alone at home. When her father the truck driver came home for a few days at a time, he acted like he had no idea who she was – let alone his wife, the woman reciting bible verses in front of the stove. *The only reason they didn't divorce during that time was because he always had an excuse to escape.* Sunny's mother tried multiple times to get her daughter involved at church, but it had never been for her. Especially since they only tentatively accepted the "sinners" of Paradise Valley because their church membership was greatly outnumbered.

This place? Where Sunny's aunt kept a respectful distance from her sister? This was where Sunny had the greatest memories of her childhood. Every summer was an excuse to pack a duffel bag and live out of a guest room if things weren't too busy. Sunny learned everything, from hospitality, to cooking, to gardening, from her aunt. Losing her to cancer had been one of the most devastating events in Sunny's life. Yet the little solace she gained when she inherited Waterlily House made up for the lost. Her aunt's spirit was always there, and soon she would have a front-row seat to Sunny's wedding.

Damn. Just the thought of it brought a few tears to Sunny's eyes.

She said goodbye to Anita around five, and the promises of dinner forced Sunny back into the house, where she would touch base with Brandy about whether they were eating together or alone. *I should go spend the night with her, anyway.* Brandelyn had been right. They would have less time together as they approached the wedding. They should get in all the cuddling they could stand now.

Sunny locked up the house and stepped into her cottage only a few yards away. *This was my aunt's home for decades.* Sunny had kept much of the décor while updating a few things here and there. Her aunt was buried at the very edge of the property, the only way the county would allow it, but a memorial urn filled with notes, dried flowers, and the colorful beads she once used to create festive ornaments for her guests to take home, stood on the mantle by the wood stove. *This is also where Brandy and I first made love, Lord help me.* How picturesque had it been when she brought Brandy back to an empty Waterlily House for a private, homemade dinner and a walk around the property? Never mind what they got up to once they were in the cottage and the door was locked.

Sunny only briefly entertained the offer to move in with Brandelyn. While she would probably change her official address to Brandy's place to make things easier, she couldn't stand the thought of abandoning her aunt's cottage. She didn't care how much her CPA Hesper Chess slyly suggested she turn it into a proper guest house to make more money. Brandy could as easily sell her house and move in here! They could build onto the cottage to make more room for them. An extra bedroom and office would be nothing with the extra, unused space behind the cottage. Was it really *so* inconvenient for the busy doctor to live a mile outside of town?

Yet Brandy was stubborn like that. Most of the time, Sunny loved how confident Brandelyn was in her opinions and resolute in her stands. But God if it didn't make for the occasional disagreement between them! How were they supposed to be a married couple if they lived in different places?

So stubborn. I'm the one who can't move as easily. I have roots here. My job is here, and I have to be on call during the busy seasons. Why did Brandy have to be like that... about so many things?

It reminded her of that little thing hanging in the back of her closet.

Sunny pulled out her overnight bag she always used when heading to Brandy's for the night. While she put in a change of underwear and a fresh T-shirt for the next day, she glanced at her half-open closet and wondered if she should indulge.

Once the idea was in her mind, she couldn't help herself. She had to open her closet all the way and push aside her jackets, long-sleeved blouses, and dress pants slung over plastic hangers.

There, zipped up in a white bag, was her wedding dress.

She gingerly brought it out and laid it on her bed. The slow descent of the zipper brought the same excitement she felt the first time she spotted this beauty hanging on the clearance rack. *Only one size too big. Otherwise, it was perfect.*

The beaded off-the-shoulder bodice dipped into a full, princessy tulle skirt that illuminated the room. Sunny plucked it up by the hanger and held it against her body as she walked toward her full-length mirror. The sunlight hit the glass from behind her. *Look at me. I look like such a girl.* Her mother, who had left her church and made peace with her daughter many years ago, would cry to see Sunny in a wedding dress. Her aunt, God rest her, would find a multitude of ways to dress it up and make it a Sunny Croker experience.

The biggest difference? Her mother would endlessly comment on how "tomboyish" Sunny was *finally* wearing a proper dress, and a bridal one, to boot! *How nice of me to fall in line...* Her aunt would simply go with the flow and not make a big deal out of anything.

Brandy was more similar to one of those women. That was the thing holding Sunny back from confessing that she had already bought a dress and wasn't interested in fulfilling every single one of Brandy's "traditional" wedding fantasies. But she felt like she had already used her biggest foot to stomp on the church idea. Did she have the guts to bring down the other foot on wearing a tux?

It's not that I think tuxes are bad, or that it wouldn't suit me... Brandelyn wasn't out of her mind thinking Sunny might prefer a tux, but it was an obnoxious assumption based on a few years of occasionally going to formal functions in simple suits (no vest, cummerbund, or tie, though) and always being annoyed with Brandy's marathons of *Say Yes to the Dress* and *Four Weddings.* Sunny had her reasons for not wanting to watch a twelfth episode in a row. None of those reasons amounted to *Wow I really hate wedding dresses and the people who wear them!*

What was supposed to cheer her up now only served to bring Sunny down. She carefully hung her dress back up in the closet. Perhaps the best medicine wasn't to obsess over her own clothing despair and to instead imagine how beautiful Brandy would be in whatever gown she chose.

It will really have to be spectacular to match her expectations. That only made it more exciting. Brandelyn in a wedding dress would be the visual highlight of their wedding. Sunny didn't mind taking a backseat to that, but sometimes, she wished Brandy would acknowledge that *Sunny* was a bride as well.

Chapter 5

BRANDELYN

Brandy hadn't a proper weekend to herself and her own interests in several weeks. Not since she and Debbie ramped up the wedding planning. Although Brandy had three-day weekends, she couldn't remember a time when every single one of those days wasn't spent doing *some* form of planning. Debbie was such a staple in Paradise Valley now that barista Heaven remembered her usual order of a nonfat hazelnut latte. Heaven also looked the other way when patrons brought their little doggies to have a treat, as long as they took the mutts outside to one of two tables set up on the sidewalk.

Main Street wasn't exactly... wide. The tiny metal bistro tables barely had enough room for cups and a plate of donuts, and that *still* left Brandy's foot hanging out in the sidewalk with not much space for pedestrians. Throw in Brutus, who made it his personal mission to happily yip at every person passing... it was a wonder Brandelyn was never asked to leave.

Brutus's leash was secured around the back of Brandy's chair. She kept him occupied with his little travel blanket, carefully coiled on the sidewalk behind her, and a bowl of water. He kept his cool as long as no other dogs passed, but as soon as Jessie Main took her German Shephard out for an afternoon run...

"Whoa!" Brandy grabbed Brutus before the German Shephard lunged. Teeth had been bared. A few snarls hit the air. Jessie snapped on her dog's leash and didn't offer a single word as they kept on running.

"I see Brutus continues to make big friends wherever he goes." Debbie offered a to-go cup full of hot tea to Brandelyn, who preferred tea to coffee on her days off. "What a good boy."

Her sarcasm was not lost on Brandy, but she was still too shot with adrenaline to say anything besides, "That gave me a fright. People really need to mind their dogs better."

Debbie gave her a look that insinuated Brandy might apply that same thinking to herself. *Excuse you, Brutus is a good boy.* He was the smartest, *cutest,* friendliest Pom in all of Oregon, and Brandelyn would be more than happy to prove it should the opportunity ever arise.

Except he loved to beg for donuts. Because once Sunny started feeding him nibbles of everything, this was what happened!

"Anyway." Debbie attempted to prop her pink binder labeled MEYER-CROKER between her gut and the edge of the tiny table. Usually, they would meet inside and do this at one of the bigger tables, but Brutus was seriously itching to get out of the house. Was it really such a bother that Debbie couldn't flip her pages at the speed of light? "You'll be so happy to know that the caterer can accommodate fifty vegetarian plates. Honestly, when I told him that you had fifty vegetarians who had RSVP'd to the wedding, he said he was used to much more!" Her canned laughter made Brutus growl beneath Brandelyn's chair.

"I've been thinking about the catering, actually." Brandy placed a poignant finger against her lips. "I know this is *so* last minute, but..." She ignored the look of "*Please God, don't do this to me,*" on Debbie's aged face. "What if we made *all* of the entrees vegetarian? It makes sense, you know? Sunny and I are both committed to having sustainable everything, as much as we can, and I saw this documentary last night about the carbon footprint of chicken farms..."

She detailed the atrocities put forth on the environment, even by the so-called "organic" and "free-range" farms. Besides, she was a doctor. She couldn't in good conscience serve *that* much meat, white or otherwise, to so many people.

"I know it might cost more, especially at the last minute," Brandy said, "but I bet if we substitute the meats for tofurkeys or whatever, nobody will notice! I had one the other day. It was actually good." Of course, it didn't beat her own turkey burgers – real turkey, of course – but didn't it make a nice alternative? She might become a vegetarian yet!

"Brandy." Great. Here came that saccharin-coated voice that meant Debbie was about to talk down to one of her clients. *I'm on to you.* Brandelyn used that same voice on her patients when they came to her after a quick perusal of the internet told them they were dying of cancer because they cut their finger. "You realize that vegetarian food still employs eggs? If you want to go vegan, we'll have to get a whole new caterer to provide that level of…"

"I *know* vegetarian food has eggs, okay?" Brandy rolled her eyes. Beneath her chair, Brutus barked his confidence in his mother's intelligence. "I'm a doctor, Debbie. I know what kind of food goes into which diet."

"Yes, well… if sustainability is your goal… wait, have you talked to your fiancée yet?"

Brandelyn sat up straight and did her best to look like that yes, she had indeed brought this up with Sunny the last time they talked about the wedding. *So maybe I had the idea while I was on my way here...* "Sunny put me in charge of the catering." And the photography. And the flowers. And God knew what else. "As long as she gets her chocolate cake at the reception, you know she'll be happy with anything."

Debbie looked as if she didn't believe that. *Tough titties. Answer my question, huh?* Brandy didn't want to deal with this. She was supposed to have a lovely afternoon hashing out the last of the details of her wedding, due to happen in about... what? Three weeks? Would they solidify the catering news or what? *I have an appointment with Meadow the florist on Monday to make sure she's got the orchids ordered.* Things really shouldn't be so complicated. Why did people think Brandy was getting this taken care of *now?*

"I can look into having more vegetarian options offered at the reception, but I'm not sure I can get them to commit to anything else right now. Was there anything else that you..."

"So about Brutus being the ring-bearer, I was thinking of instead of forcing all that fur into a little tux, we go with a bowtie and *maybe* a clip-on top hat." Brandelyn turned up the charm with a dazzling smile. "What do you think? I've already been working with him in the evenings." The first thing Brandelyn did after coming back from her walks with Brutus was teach him how to trot down the aisle with a little pillow of rings on his back. So far, they were only to the pillow stage, but Brandy had confidence that her little Brutie would steal the show at her wedding. Until she walked down the aisle, anyway.

"It is certainly ideal to *not* put animals in costumes at a wedding ceremony, yes." Debbie continued to talk through her teeth. She looked a lot like Brutus when he didn't want to give up the toy in his mouth. "You know, Brandy, I've dealt with animals in ceremonies before. I can think of only one occasion where it went off without a hitch, but that was a former show dog that did tricks like that for half its life. I usually suggest that we *not* go with motifs that don't include any rational human thought. I'm sure Brutus is very clever..."

"I taught him to shake hands in one hour."

Debbie briefly closed her eyes to compose herself. "Be that as it may, I seriously ask you to reconsider including your dog in the ceremony. I'm sure it would be fine if he's there to share in your big day with Sunny, but I wouldn't have him playing a key part. Besides, do you want him detracting from your big wedding gown reveal?"

Brandelyn hated to admit that she *had* considered that. "My dress definitely wouldn't look good picking up dog hair off the runner, no."

`"How about I come up with some ideas on how Brutus can participate, hm?" Debbie's smile made Brandy want to reach across the table and smack her. *Don't be so condescending to me... I'm the one paying you!* "No training involved. Besides maybe a sit and stay, perhaps." She flipped to another page in her folder. Brandelyn narrowed her eyes, grateful that Debbie couldn't see the scorn behind a pair of thick sunglasses. Beneath the chair, Brutus continued to growl on behalf of his mother's honor. "Now, how about we go over the cake details? We still have yet to decide on the perfect cake topper."

Debbie presented her with two pre-made albums, each one a variant of *"lesbian weddings."* Brandy didn't know what irked her more: that one flip-book was filled with two women in dresses, or the other was a dress and tux... with the figure in the tux only looking *vaguely* feminine. They might as well have been the male figurines!

"Sunny is wearing a tux, as you know." Brandelyn didn't know why she was presented with both options, honestly. Who was the one that referred Sunny to the tux shop? Debbie. Who was the one that ensured the tailors would adhere to the colors of white and pink? *Debbie.* "Do you have any 'grooms' with a pink cummerbund?" Brandy half-expected to get another roll of the eyes. Instead, she was treated to a "groom" with pink wrapped around "his" midsection.

It was totally the wrong shade, but it was a good start. Yet Brandelyn couldn't stop thinking that it truly highlighted the stark difference between the bride in her porcelain princess gown and the ambiguously-gendered person in a suit and pink cummerbund. *Sunny deserves better than this.* Whatever cake topper they used should represent both of their personalities, let alone appearances! Her sandy blond hair could not be thoroughly represented by a male figurine with brown hair. Yet the blond ones highlighted the masculine features that did *not* look like Sunny at all! Her heart-shaped face, soft curves, and kindly brown eyes were nowhere to be seen in these booklets. Brandelyn had no qualms picking the first brunette bride standing proudly on her wedding, but she would be damned if her guests looked at her cake topper and wondered what *guy* she was marrying!

"No, none of these will do." Shaking her head, Brandelyn closed the book and opened the one with two brides in wedding gowns. She might as well look. Maybe it would take the bad taste now forming on her tongue. "They don't look anything like Sunny. I know you haven't *seen* her much, but..."

"I know what she looks like," Debbie said through gritted teeth. "There is one in the book you have there..."

Brandelyn paused on the page Debbie looked at with a little fondness. "Is this the one?" Brandy pointed to the two brides holding hands, both in identical gowns, but their bouquets a lovely degree of red and pink. The bride on the right had her dark hair up in the bun with the kind of ringlets Brandy considered for her matrimonial fashion. The blonde must have had long hair pulled back into a ponytail, but looking at her from the front, it was easy to imagine she kept it close to her skull.

It looked like Sunny. Or as close as porcelain or plastic could come.

"Too bad she's not wearing a dress," Debbie said with a sigh. "Unless you think she might be offended by a topper with a dress..."

"You know how she is." Brandy closed the book. "I haven't seen her wear a dress in all the years I've known her. Hm. Except for that one time. Except it was a long time ago, and she's said so herself that she doesn't like skirts." Sometimes Sunny wore a long, cotton skirt on the hottest days of the year, but she kept them to the Waterlily House and claimed to favor them only because of the ventilation. Brandelyn had never questioned her about it. Why would she? Some women wore skirts. Others didn't for whatever reason. What was it to her? She reminded *both* her female and male patients that they should keep certain body parts regularly aired out and free from constricting pants. Honestly, it didn't matter what they kept in those pants. Proper ventilation was important! *The amount of chafing and the number of infections I've seen...*

"Are you all right?" Debbie asked, as soon as Brandy shuddered in her seat.

"Oh, absolutely peachy." *Just thinking about yeast infections. Don't mind me.* The worst part about being the only doctor in town was walking around the grocery store and thinking, *"Your yeast infection was the worst I've ever seen! And* your *rash was totally preventable if you used that after-sex cream I prescribed you. God, have you started proper hygiene routines yet? If half this town knew you didn't wash your you-know-what..."* "I'm sorry I'm so difficult, Debbie. But I recognize that this isn't only *my* wedding. Sunny may have put most of it in my hands, but I want to make sure she's properly represented as well. For God's sake, she's the reason we're having it at Waterlily House." Compromising on the chapel wedding of her dreams was one of the hardest things Brandy had ever done, but she knew how much the B&B meant to Sunny. Besides, Sunny's arguments that they weren't religious and that it would be much cheaper to have both the ceremony and reception in a place they didn't have to rent were sound. Didn't mean Brandelyn *liked* them, but they made sense. *Still, I always wanted to be like Princess Di walking down that aisle with church pews full of people...* When she watched Kate Middleton walk down the aisle at Westminster Abbey, Brandelyn's eyes were full of tears. It was the most beautiful sight she had seen since she was four!

She would chase another dream for Sunny. Waterlily House *was* a picturesque location for any wedding, and Brandy came around to the idea of an outdoor ceremony when she double-checked Paradise Valley's historical records for weather at the end of June. Perfect temperatures – not too hot yet and cool in the evenings – and little rain after the start of June. The morning might be foggy, but that was why they scheduled the ceremony for two in the afternoon. They didn't need to do earlier when the guests could migrate straight to the reception a few yards away. *That reminds me, I need to check in with those Port-a-John rentals.* Three hundred people were not about to share the four bathrooms in Waterlily House. The fewer people coming in and out of there, the better.

Besides, Waterlily House was where they shared their first kiss! Their first night together! It was the perfect romantic place for their nuptials. Who cared about some stuffy church they had never been to before? If there were a God, He could as easily come bless their vows outside in his own creation!

"I'll keep my eye out for a proper cake topper," Debbie said. "You and Sunny might also consider one that doesn't depict people at all. Is there a symbol that is important to your relationship? Many couples go with hearts these days. Or a symbol from their cultures. Ooh, have I shown you the photo of this one couple who had an elaborate, beaded sculpture created for their cake? It's a bit last minute for something like that, but we could search for a pre-made one that..."

"I'd prefer people." Lest anyone forget who the stars of the wedding were.

Still, it was the first time Brandelyn considered Sunny in a wedding dress. It might be a pleasant sight, since Sunny had the perfect cheekbones, bust, and hips for a nice dress. But it was so unlike her! The concept of her wearing a wedding dress had never crossed Brandy's mind before, and she wasn't about to bring it up. Besides, the image Brandelyn had always envisioned was *wedding dress and tuxedo.* That's how it was when one went traditional. Who was to say that lesbians could not be traditional? Wasn't it a bigger kick in the teeth to the patriarchy and all things oppressive if Sunny showed up in a tux and claimed her bride?

"Brandy?" Debbie sweetly said. "Are you there? Where have you gone? We have a few things to go over still."

Whoops. Brandelyn always did fall into fantasy when she imagined her fiancée being her usual badass self.

Chapter 6

SUNNY

"Do you need this for next year?" Sunny held up a red and green Christmas streamer made of construction paper. Knowing Anita, the English teacher put it up around Christmastime and never bothered to take it down again before the end of the year. When posters of Shakespeare, Maya Angelou, and Jane Austen already covered the walls, a harried teacher was not wont to consider what might come down after the second semester began. "Because if you don't, I might steal it for my Christmas decorations this year."

"It goes in the orange tote!" Anita called from outside her opened classroom door. The windows were likewise open, allowing the cool, late spring air filter through the stuffy classroom. *This place sure is quiet without a hundred students running around.* Clark High School served the towns of Paradise Valley and Roundabout, but that didn't mean a large population of students to recruit. The school district was lucky to have a hundred high schoolers at any moment. One hundred and twenty during a good year. *When I graduated, we had eighty in the whole school.* Her class had been a humble nineteen students. Even now, when wandering the hallways and looking at portraits of classes past, she noted that hers was one of the smallest. Anita's, meanwhile, boasted a whole twenty-three! *Someone's class had fewer dropouts than mine.* Sunny would never forget the scandal when two of her female classmates dropped out because they got pregnant at the same time. It hadn't been a pact of any kind, but when they discovered their kids had the same father? Anarchy.

The orange tote Anita had referred to currently sat on a desk near the front of the classroom, and was already stuffed with seasonal decorations like Styrofoam jack-o-lanterns and paper snowflakes. Anita apparently had construction paper streamers for every season, but she never bothered to put up the third and fourth semester ones. Shame. That yellow and pink for spring was really pretty.

Anita returned a few seconds later, her long white skirt swishing against the linoleum that had covered the floors of Clark High School since they were teenagers. She hooked a clear bin beneath her arm and pulled the cursive letters off their perches above the whiteboard. *That's a recent addition. Never forget the screech of chalk against a blackboard.* Sunny didn't have a lot of nostalgia for her school years, but she definitely had *memories.* Like the senior prank that included a mountain of opened Skittles dumped across the main entrance. *We made the freshmen pick them up, one by one!* They couldn't get away with that now. Sunny was surprised to walk in a few years ago and see a giant sign by the secretary's office that said, *"How To Be A Good Person. #1) Bullying and Hazing Are Not Tolerated..."* Apparently, they had to spell it out now.

Still, being a teacher wasn't easy. It couldn't have been, since not only did Sunny remember how she tormented her own teachers – some of them *still* around – but she heard the horror stories from Ms. Tichenor. When Sunny asked about the giant chunk of whiteboard missing, Anita explained that one of her students went "freakin' nuts" about his parents' divorce and ripped it out when her back was turned. That was considered a good day.

"What are we doing with the Holy Trinity?" Sunny asked, referring to the posters.

"I have to remove *everything.*"

"That's so dumb. Did teachers do that when we were kids?" Sunny hopped up on a stool and undid the pushpin holding Billy Shakes to the wall. He unceremoniously limped forward as gravity took hold.

"No. It's a more recent policy that we take everything down over the summer. In case they want to shuffle the classrooms around again."

"How often does that happen?"

"Every other year, at least."

Sunny rolled her eyes. She also rolled up the poster of Shakespeare and gingerly tucked him into a tube she found in another tote. "Change for change's sake, it sounds like."

"They're 'revolutionizing' education with a shoestring budget, okay?"

"I pay taxes," Sunny muttered. "So why the hell does this school have no budget, and why can't I drive to Brandy's house without hitting three potholes?"

"That's a question for Dave, the history and government teacher." Anita chuckled. "Thanks again for helping me out today, Sun. I know you're really busy with your house and the wedding, but I appreciate it. This always takes me twice as long to do by myself."

It's the least I could do after you helped me with my gardening. "I had to get out of town for a while," she said, referring to how Clark High stood right between Paradise Valley and Roundabout. As a child, she never thought about how weird it was to see a high school out in the middle of nowhere. Now, though, she realized that many aspects of her childhood were "different." Not even Brandelyn totally understood how a school could be outside of city limits. *I'm honestly surprised a big city childhood like that led her to being comfortable in rural Oregon.* Brandy claimed to have grown accustomed to a quieter life when going to school in OHSU. Still, how did a big city woman become a small town doctor? It was one of those bits about Brandelyn that Sunny would continue to discover for the rest of her life.

"Is the Bridezilla still on the prowl?" Anita dropped her smile. "Sorry. I shouldn't call her that. Oh, and make sure Maya goes on top, would you? She gets the spot of honor."

"Two women on top of the most celebrated male writer in history. Got it."

"Always thought that was Rumi," Anita said.

"Who?"

"Never mind. Come sit in on one of my classes sometime, huh? I should get a Rumi poster..."

Sunny made sure that the poster of Maya Angelou was on top. "It's okay to call Brandy a Bridezilla. She kinda acts like one. Then again, it's her dream we're enacting. She can have almost anything she wants."

"Lord, is that what you're telling yourself? I thought some of the things I overheard teenagers saying was *bad*."

Sunny jerked upright. "How is it bad?" she asked. "You know I've never had big marriage or wedding aspirations. Hell, remember when you asked me to be your +1 at your sister's wedding? I almost bailed, because I honestly hate other people's weddings."

"I thought you bailed because you couldn't decide between a suit or a dress?"

"That's why I ended up going with a blouse and slacks." It had come in handy many times since. Sunny needed to dress up for something semi-formal? Slacks and blouse! It was the perfect blend of sticking with what she found comfortable while also avoiding strange comments. Not everyone in Paradise Valley or the general area was used to women wearing suits and tuxedos. They thought that kind of thing only happened at lesbian weddings. *Never forget Anita's uncle, who asked us if two women getting married always meant two suits... because we're obviously trying to be men, or something.* Sunny was really getting tired of the gender politics over a simple outfit. Why couldn't she wear something that was comfortable, while still looking nice? Comfort didn't always mean *physical.*

Anita's silence spoke volumes. She had clearly heard her friend's response. Her choice to not say anything was basically screaming, *"You keep telling yourself that."*

"Besides," Sunny continued, "we're getting married at Waterlily House, which was the most important thing to me. You have no idea how much Brandy had to concede her desires for that chapel vision. She watched way too many religious weddings growing up."

"So did we," Anita said. "Yet somehow we're not ragin' to get married in churches."

"People are different, yeah? To her, the chapel wasn't about being Christian or getting married in front of God. It was all about the aesthetic ingrained into her since she first realized she really, really loves weddings."

"If you say so."

"You're the one calling her Bridezilla."

"Because I've heard *so* many stories about her and that wedding planner of yours. I heard she was asking about that dog of hers being the ring bearer?"

"Who did you hear that from?" Sunny asked. "Because it's not *that* true."

"If you say so!"

"Would you stop saying that?"

Sunny hadn't meant to snap at her friend, especially since she came all this way to help Anita pack up her classroom at the end of the year, but she was getting tired of people acting like Brandelyn stomped all over her. Did people think Brandy was the Queen Bee of the relationship? *Hardly. We have complementary personality types.* They got along because Brandy was a go-getter and Sunny knew how to slow down and take in the flowers. She loved to think that they were beautiful opposites like that. The kind who, on the surface, didn't get along. But when one dug deeper and made things work, it was a balanced relationship to last a lifetime.

"Sorry," Anita finally said. "I know things are stressful right now. Just don't let your fiancée walk all over you *and* make every single decision. Don't want you showing up to your wedding and having no idea what's going on."

"I think I would know if she suddenly went with a space or an aquarium theme," Sunny muttered. *Not that Brandelyn would* ever *do that*. It went totally against her traditional mindset. *I'm the one who would suggest an under the sea theme. Ahem.* More like flowers for days, but whatever. "Well, there might be one thing that's been bugging me."

"Hm?"

Anita was filled with rapt attention as soon as her friend announced something may be up. Unsurprising, wasn't it? She lived for this kind of drama. She really was an English teacher!

"She's so convinced that I want to wear a tux that she's focused so much of our planning on it. She's picking out a cake topper right now, and I know she's going to choose one that has me represented by a guy in a suit." Sighing, Sunny continued, "It fits into her vision, you know? She wants to be the beautiful bride on the arm of a handsome person in a tux."

"Do you not want to do that?"

See? Even Anita was surprised that Sunny might not want to be confined to a suit for her wedding. *I really project the whole butch thing better than I thought.* Which was funny, since she never personally called herself butch. Not out loud, anyway. She was simply... Sunny. A woman who liked jeans, short hair, and a no-nonsense life. That described half the women, gay or straight, in Oregon.

"I may or may not have already bought a dress before this all came out," Sunny muttered.

"Huh? What was that?"

Anita didn't sound that way to be sarcastic. She had genuinely not heard Sunny, because Sunny didn't want to be heard. If she told her best friend the truth, then it was like pulling back the mask to reveal the scars. Everything felt much too late now. She had her chance to speak up, and had let it pass. Sunny might as well embrace the inevitable.

"I said I've bought a dress already."

"Whoa. Really?"

Anita dropped the decoration in her hand. Was it really so impossible to imagine Sunny in a wedding dress? Or was this all done for comedic effect at her expense? What was so wrong with her wanting to look like a bride alongside her fiancée? Maybe *she* had some visions that extended beyond Waterlily House. How could something that seemed so simple to her completely rock people off their foundations?

"It was sort of spur of the moment." Sunny sat on one of the desks, feet in the chair as she detangled one of the colorful streamers in the orange tote. "I didn't mean to buy a dress, really, but when I saw it on the clearance rack..."

"Wait, so you actually went into a bridal boutique and sifted through the clearance rack?" Anita put her hands on her hips, as if she were about to scold one of her students. "Here I thought you fell in love with a dress on a mannequin in a store window. Anyway, go on."

The desk rocked beneath the force of Sunny's scoff. "I was curious to see what they had! Brandy and I had recently gotten engaged, and I felt the whole wedding thing until I realized it really wasn't for me and that she should do it. I was compelled to go into a shop in the city. Most of it wasn't really my thing until I started sifting through the clearance rack. Suddenly a $200 dress that only needs a few alterations doesn't seem so bad. I tried it on and..."

"You said yes to the dress, huh?" Anita slapped her hand on Sunny's shoulder. The desk rocked some more. "When were you going to tell me about this?"

"I haven't told anyone. It's been my secret shame ever since."

"Brandy really doesn't know, huh?"

"No. I have no idea how to tell her. If I ever do." Maybe she would donate the dress to a charity that could resell it to a woman who desperately needed it more than Sunny did.

"Brandelyn's so wrapped up in me wearing a tuxedo to match her image that..."

Anita didn't hesitate to cut her off mid-sentence. "You have to tell her."

"What?"

Shoulders squared and face grim, Anita turned her friend toward her. "You can't start your marriage off like this. Are you crazy? Keeping something like this from Brandy, never asserting yourself about what is most important to you... that's how you start a marriage off with her shoe treads all over your back. It's only going to get worse. Because as soon as you're married, she's going to take everything she's ever learned about you over the years and use that as the *base* of your interactions. Trust me. I've seen it happen before."

"Says the woman who's never been married."

"I've been in a committed relationship *way* longer than you. For Bonnie and me, it was moving in together that brought it out in us. Let me tell you, having seen a lot of couples get married over the years? Doesn't matter if you're gay or straight. Shit changes. You don't have to change your last name or move across the country to feel it."

Sunny hated to admit that her best friend was right. She had left her spine somewhere beneath the floorboards of Waterlily House, and she best dig it out again before it was too late.

She simply didn't know where she had stowed her hammer.

Chapter 7

BRANDELYN

It took one day and two rental vans to haul Brandelyn's extended family from the airport to her house in Paradise Valley. Why they insisted on coming two weeks before the wedding, Brandy could never guess, but she knew she would never again have peace until her honeymoon.

Two vans full of Meyers? She might as well ask for a lifetime supply of Tylenol.

"Lizzie?" her mother, Mrs. Cathy Meyer, shouted toward the third row. Brandy's sister looked up from her phone. Between the first and third rows, a handful of Meyers bickered about the type of trees growing alongside the highway. All Brandy knew was that they were wrong. "How are those bagels holding up? You know I don't like my bagels soggy!"

Lizzie didn't try to look in the bag holding the precious bagels Cathy insisted on bringing from New York. Supposedly, there was one for every day she would be in Oregon. *Only my mother would pull a stunt like that.* "They're fine, Mom!"

With a huff, Cathy threw herself into the passenger seat and motioned for Brandelyn to pay attention to her. "If you weren't driving, I'd tell you to go check for me."

"There are plenty of decent bagels around here. We can stop at the Safeway and get you some fresh ones before we get home."

"What the hell is 'the Safeway'? Is that like the Pig in the Blanket they have down in the south? Because I had those so-called bagels from the Pig in the Blanket when we went down to Helena, Georgia, and they *were not bagels.*"

"I think you mean Piggly-Wiggly, Mom." *What if I told her they used to have them here in Oregon?* "The bagels here are fine. I have them all the time."

"Because you've grown soft in Ore-gone!"

Brandelyn cringed at her mother's blatant mispronunciation of the state some of them now called home. "I suggest you don't call it that while you're here, Mom. The locals are a bit touchy about tourists mispronouncing things."

"I'm no tourist! I'm your mother! Lizzie!" Cathy's voice was so loud that she silenced her grandson screaming out license plate numbers as they went by. "Where did you say your friend went to school around here, again? Will-uh-mutt College?"

"It's Willamette, damnit," Brandelyn muttered beneath her breath. Then, louder, "Could you call your husband in the other van and tell him I need to pull over up here to get some gas? They barely gave me half a tank at the rental place."

Cathy begrudgingly did her duty as Brandelyn came upon the Pump-And-Go. Everyone over the age of sixteen balked at the price of gas out in rural Oregon, which was compounded when Brandelyn pulled up to the pump, cut the engine, and rolled down the window.

"Oh, dear, it really is warm in here." Cathy fanned herself with the road map she plucked from PDX. "Maybe we should get us some ice cream while you fill up the tank."

The station attendant popped out of his booth, orange warning vest flickering in the sunlight. He tipped his hat to Brandy, who hung out the window to order her gas.

"Oh, no, dear," Cathy scoffed beside her. "We don't need full service for a *rental.*"

Brandelyn handed the attendant her rewards card. "Fill it with regular, please." She turned to her mother as soon as the attendant grabbed the pump, much to the amusement of everyone in the van. "This is Oregon, Mom. You can't pump your own gas."

"Whoa," her oldest nephew Matthew said. "It's like New Jersey!"

Cathy informed her grandson that Oregon was *nothing* like New Jersey. Whether that was a good or bad thing, Brandelyn could only guess. "Well, that's ridiculous," she said to her daughter. "It's no wonder your gas prices are so damn high when you're paying people to do things you can perfectly well do yourself!"

"Do you, like..." Lizzie began in the far back row, "do they, like, touch your car whether you want them to or not?"

"Obviously," Brandelyn said.

"Remind me to never move to Oregon. Or New Jersey."

"You guys are so particular."

Brandy might as well have told them all they smelled like rancid BO and couldn't recite the Pledge of Allegiance if they tried. When the attendant returned five minutes later, it was to a van full of women and children arguing over *who,* exactly, was particular, and *who,* exactly, was a big ol' dumb butt who wouldn't last two days back in Brooklyn. Someone might have to pump her own gas.

I'm regretting this already. It was one thing to go home for a visit and be treated to the family that never shut up. It was quite another to bring them to her new home, let alone her *literal* home. While it wasn't the first time either her mother or sister visited, Brandy never had her whole family, from parents to cousins, in her house at once. *At least they can amuse each other while I'm working or doing wedding stuff.* Cathy would insist on visiting the clinic to give her expert opinion on décor and bedside manner. Lizzie would spend half her days in the antique shops and the library. Her cousin Monica would run around town looking for a decent Wi-Fi hotspot, not because she had to study or conduct business, but because her biggest hobby was writing a blog nobody ever visited. (Except for Brandelyn. One time. With regret.)

Their reactions to Paradise Valley were always of overexaggerated shock. "How can this place be so tiny?" Monica croaked. "Have you ever seen so many butch haircuts in your life?" asked Lizzie. "How can you get any services in a tiny town like this?" That was the thing Cathy cared about the most. "Do you have a post office? Where the hell is a Bank of America ATM? There's only *one* place to get pizza around here? You must be kidding. This place thinks it's the Catskills but it's really no better than Appalachia!"

Yet their criticisms soon turned to gasps of shock and awe when they beheld Brandy's house on Florida Street. "Such Victorian charm! Were these really built in the Victorian era?" Lizzie grabbed her sons' hands and hauled them toward Brandelyn's door. "I didn't think Oregon existed back then."

Take a history class, sis. Seriously. Did these people overlook the state's founding date on the flag? There were five flags on Main Street alone. "I think these houses were built in the '80s. Mine was." She had bought it from a nice elderly couple who were downsizing and moving to the central coast. They had no need for four bedrooms, three bathrooms, and a country kitchen. Nor could the one forever recovering from pneumonia bother with the yard anymore. Granted, Brandelyn didn't need that many bedrooms, either, but at least she had the excuse for "growing a family" with Sunny. Whatever that entailed.

"Oh my *God,* it's the baby!" Cathy squealed to behold Brutus, ready for his afternoon walk. A neighbor should have stopped by earlier to let him out into the backyard for a run, but by the way he wagged his tail and slapped his nails against the hardwood floors, he hadn't walked more than five feet in five days. "Who's Grandma's little fluffy butt, hm? Who's a good boy and wants a treat?'

Cathy opened her purse and dumped a bag of dog treats onto the floor. Her grandsons and nephew tore up the stairs to claim their room. Brandy's stepfather ambled in with half the luggage, sweating like it was a hundred. Monica lamented that there was no air conditioning built into the house. (When somebody told her she could open a window, she balked.) Lizzie went straight into the kitchen and moaned that her sister had the wrong kind of milk. She was supposed to have *almond* milk, not coconut! Where was the nearest grocery store? Three bucks should do it, right?

The next time somebody asked Brandy why her family came two weeks early for the wedding, she would point to this mess and say, "It takes them two weeks to adjust to a small town on the west coast." Everyone fought over the TV within two seconds, and the screaming didn't stop once they realized that Brandelyn didn't have the fabled satellite service they heard so much about. It was Hulu and Netflix or bust.

"How is my husband going to watch the Mets while he's here?" Cathy scoffed as she followed her daughter into the kitchen. "Would you hate it if he installed the ESPN app and logged into his account?"

"He can do about anything he wants that doesn't get me charged, Mom."

"I should hope so. Your stepfather is going to be bored out of his mind while we women get on with this wedding business. Now, where is your dress? I wanna see it!"

Brutus nipped at their heels and danced around the upstairs hallway. Three boys argued over who slept in the bed in their room and who was stuck on an air mattress. Brandelyn's stepfather's coughing started the moment he settled onto the couch and shouted that he didn't know how to download the ESPN app onto the TV. Monica rushed into the master bedroom to ask for the Wi-Fi password. Lizzie was already in the backyard smoking a cigarette.

Not once did anyone mention Sunny or ask where she was. It took Brandy about an hour to realize that, and by then, her family had firmly settled into petty arguments over blankets and bachelorette parties.

Chapter 8

SUNNY

The most inconvenient thing about getting married at the height of tourist season wasn't blocking out B&B reservations for that week. It was telling nice old men like Mr. Murray that, no, the house wouldn't be available at *all* until well after Fourth of July.

"You mean you don't have anyone running the place at all while you're gone?" The wiry man with stark white hair and a collared shirt always tucked into his jeans followed Sunny into the kitchen, where she prepped the coffee pot for the afternoon. The landscaper that came by once a month rode by the window on his lawnmower. Between him and Mr. Murray,

Sunny was liable to have a stress-related heart attack.

"The whole place is totally shut down while I'm off on my honeymoon, I'm afraid." Sunny offered her regular guest a smile. "I don't really have anyone to run it while I'm gone. Nobody I trust enough, anyway." She turned that fake smile into a genuine grin. "If you book now, though, I'm sure you can get a room somewhere for the Fourth of July celebrations, if that's what you're worried about."

"It's not so much that, Miss Sunny." He always called her that, and she always called him Mr. Murray. Seemed weird to call the kindly old retired professor anything else. The man was hard at work on both a memoir and an original novel about the Portland underground. He rented a room for a few days every month, declaring Paradise Valley the best place to get away from the metro area and "just write." Indeed, he was usually hard at work typing on his Chromebook or writing longhand in a notebook. The stacks of books he brought from the libraries – both in Paradise Valley and from

Portland – confused some of other guests, who sometimes thought they belonged to Waterlily House. When Sunny informed him that the house would be closed while she was on her honeymoon, he looked as lost as the occasional bear wandering into the yard. "It's... I'm not sure where to go now..."

Sunny turned away from the coffee maker. Poor Mr. Murray was so defeated that he had removed his bifocals. "Now, I know for a fact you've been talking about going to Astoria for a bit of change."

"Well, yes..."

"I truly appreciate your continued patronage, Mr. Murray." Sunny went as far as to put a gentle hand on his arm, which made him blush and look away in that infallible politeness of his. "You know how rare it is for me to get out of town for a while. Sometimes I have somebody take over the place, but for my honeymoon, I think I'd like to not have to worry about it." Anita would be driving by every other day to keep an eye on things, but Sunny wasn't about to ask her to run the place in her absence.

Not even with young Leigh Ann volunteering at her side. *That would be awkward, anyway. Leigh Ann is one of Anita's students.* It was already weird enough that Leigh Ann knew Sunny was best friends with the high school English teacher.

"You really do deserve a break, Miss Sunny."

"Gonna be Mrs. Sunny soon!"

"Indeed! And a doctor!" Mr. Murray's chuckles meant he was about to put his bifocals back on his face. "Well, I'll figure something out for my Fourth of July excursion. Like you said, I've been meaning to give Astoria another chance. I only worry it might be crazy over the Fourth of July, too. Sometimes these small towns take it more seriously than anyone in the city."

Sunny was about to suggest a town on the coast when she was summoned by the phone ringing next to the fridge. Mr. Murray excused himself from the kitchen. Sunny bypassed the sign asking guests to please not answer the phone if she was around. Likewise, local calls were free, but long distance required a small fee. Since service was still spotty out there for some cell phone types, it remained a pertinent reminder to keep an eye on the landline.

Especially if it were ringing!

"Hello, you have reached Waterlily House. This is Sunny speaking." Sunny was alone by the time she answered. Good. Mr. Murray might be a bit miffed to know what happened next.

"Sunny, is it?" The woman on the other end was as no-nonsense as the wedding planner. "This is Dahlia Granger from Hibiscus Films. I believe I emailed you the other day? I hadn't heard a response, so I'm calling to follow up."

"Hibiscus..." Yes, Sunny recalled some of that. She had in fact received a reservation request for the whole of Waterlily House for most of July. *I haven't had the chance to look it over.* Mostly because she was so busy with the rest of her life and business. A reservation for all of July? When she would be gone for part of it? She might as well be asked to play the role of King Solomon between an unknown entity and her quiet regulars.

Still, that was a lot of money...

"Yes," Sunny eventually said. "I do believe I received your reservation request the other day, but didn't have the time to go over it yet. How can I help you, Ms. Granger?"

"Well, as stipulated in the request, my crew and I will be in Paradise Valley next month for some filming. There are four of us, and we should like to rent three to four rooms from you for most of July. I'm not sure exactly how long we'll be there for, but we're arriving into town on the second."

Lovely. Two days after the wedding. Because Sunny would totally be around for that. "Yes, that's part of the snafu, I suppose."

"Oh, are you already booked? Mayor Rath assured me that you usually have a couple rooms available at any time."

Thank you, Ms. Mayor. If Karen kept it up, she would soon have people believing that all of Paradise Valley was losing business by the month. "Actually, I'm getting married at the end of this month and shall be on my honeymoon for the first chunk of July."

"Oh! I had no idea. Congratulations." Before Sunny could accept any congratulations, however, the prospective guest continued. "Are you saying that you won't be open for part of that time? Could you refer me to any of the other fine establishments in your area that may be able to accommodate us? I must admit, it's been a bit of a trial to figure this part of our project out, because there seem to be few lodges in the area."

"Especially in July," Sunny further explained. "It's a big tourist season around here, yes." Those who didn't come only for the Fourth of July festivities often lingered or returned for Paradise Pride at the end of the month. That was the *real* party, and both Brandy and Sunny agreed to be back in time for it. There was usually a small to-do for newlyweds, and they didn't want to miss out on their free goodies. "Well, I hadn't planned on being open, but if it's only the four of you, I may be able to open those rooms for you. You must keep in mind, however, that it might only be part-timed staffed during the day, so you would be on your own for most of it." Poor Anita was about to be roped into some adventure over the course of her summer vacation. *At least Leigh Ann will have something to do.* Last Sunny heard, the student hadn't lined up a job for the break. She needed *something* to keep her preoccupied.

"We mostly keep to ourselves, and any time spent at the house would be working on our film. We've looked into renting a proper house elsewhere, but there don't seem to be many up for short-term rentals. Air BnB was really quite sad."

Especially in Summer, yes. Sunny would be repeating that until the point was driven into Dahlia's head. "I can give you a group rate. It will help mitigate my inability to be there the first part of the month to offer the usual breakfast, but as long as you sign a cleaning waiver and pay a small deposit, you can have free range of the kitchen to make your meals." She remembered the Halcyon days when she didn't need a deposit to use the damn kitchen. "I'll have to take a close look at my calendar. If you can send me some more concrete dates, I can figure something out."

"Thank you *so* much." Dahlia sighed in relief. "We can list you as one of our sponsors at the end of our film about Paradise Valley."

Film about Paradise Valley? Sunny scrunched her nose. She hadn't heard anything about that. Wouldn't a movie being made in town make the news? Hell, those camera crews showing up last April to stalk Jalen had created such a stir that they made front page of the newspaper. Was Sunny out of the loop because of the wedding planning? She needed to go into town more often. The summer was really bad for avoiding town, due to the great weather keeping her in the outdoors and a booming business preoccupying her time with guests. The wedding only made her more detached from the gossip around town.

"What exactly is this film about?" Sunny braved asking.

"Oh, we're filming a small documentary for local interests." The way Dahlia said it made Sunny still think that there was something more to it, but that was the official statement they were handing out to the townsfolk. "I assure you this isn't Hollywood or anything. We're not planning to make the rounds at Cannes, if that's what you're wondering!"

Sunny didn't really believe it, but what could she say? She was better off agreeing to take a look at the reservation while wondering what she would say to Anita and Leigh Ann. At least she could give Anita a small stipend for taking over for a few days. Leigh Ann might riot, however, and Sunny would need at least *one* person on hand.

Why oh why did things have to be so complicated lately? Sunny merely wanted to plan her wedding and think of a nice life together with the woman she loved. A woman she hadn't seen very often since the future in-laws came into town. Sunny had made the required drop-by to say hello and be fawned over, but the Meyers were often wrapped up in their own world of petty arguments and cheek kisses that made up for all the heavy words said only five minutes ago.

It explained a lot about Brandelyn, really. Enough that Sunny could appreciate the different perspective, and hope it meant the slightest bit of difference to how they related to one another in their marriage.

After thinking that, Sunny conceded it was a pipe dream. Some would say she was addicted to those pipes, anyway.

***

"You have *no* idea how nice this is," Brandy said, flopping down onto Sunny's loveseat in her small living room. "My house became a war zone the moment everyone flew in from New York. Be grateful you don't have to deal with your family for another week."

Sunny finished folding her laundry by the TV. The new report from Portland meant nothing to them, but Sunny was grateful she didn't have to drive around the city. "My family is also a lot more well-behaved than yours."

"You can say that again," Brandelyn muttered. "My mother attempted to barge right into one of my appointments today! Can you believe it?"

"Yes, actually."

Brandy continued, "I had to wait for my receptionist to intervene. I was busy explaining to a patient that... well, I shouldn't tell you. Just know that my mother didn't understand why she doesn't have a right to barge into my exam rooms for any reason. Doesn't matter if I'm with a patient or not! Who does that?"

"Your mother. What did she want, anyway?"

"Something about my sister's maid-of-honor dress. Apparently, the hem is not to her liking, and my mom was going to proudly announce that she was taking it in herself."

Sunny rolled her eyes. How could she express how grateful she was that her mother-in-law wasn't her responsibility?

"Sorry to dump all this on you while you're trying to get your chores done." Brandy dragged her hands down her face. *That looks like it feels nice.* Sunny would have to do it to herself when her fiancée wasn't looking. "I'm going nuts. I knew I was going to go nuts, but it's quite a difference between thinking about it theoretically... and, oh, boom, there they are! My stepfather has been complaining about my lack of cable or satellite ever since he sat down. He's a channel flipper. He hates streaming, because it forces him to choose something to watch.

"Don't ever tell him about playlists."

"That *still* takes the 'magic' out of it, I guess."

Sunny shook her head while folding the final towel. "Your family. I'm so glad they live on the other side of the country."

"They're gonna be your family soon!"

"You're sure right, Brandy." Sunny stood up, pile of towels in her arms. "Are you staying the night tonight? Or would that be too scandalous for your devoutly Jewish mother?"

"She's about as devout as a Catholic priest in Miami for spring break," Brandelyn muttered. "She wouldn't have any room to talk about us sleeping together for one night before the wedding." *Only one?* Sunny wouldn't have it. "When Lizzie was dating her boyfriend, they totally slept together – while my mother knew about it, mind you – when home from college for Christmas break. You ask me? That's when their oldest was conceived."

"You know better than most how weird parents can get."

"Even better when you make it gay, right?"

"Yup. Don't get me started on all the snide remarks I've been hearing about town."

"Hey, Bran…" Sunny stopped in front of her fiancée, still dramatically passed out on the loveseat. "You've told your parents you're marrying *me*, right?"

"You want to talk about weird parents? How about them knowing and accepting that their daughter's a lesbian, but being weirded out by a whole small town of lesbians? Then again, my mom's dying without her precious bagels."

"What's wrong with the bagels around here? Safeway always has them on sale."

"You don't understand a New Yorker's relationship to bagels. You just don't."

"Forgive me if I don't try to understand it." Sunny chuckled. "Have you exposed her to the wonders that is Paradise Pizza yet?"

"It's not New York style, so you can imagine how that went."

"So, you have the type of New Yorker parents that can't stand it when things aren't New York?"

"Sun, you've *been* to New York City with me. You know how people get there!"

Oh, Sunny remembered. She remembered so well that Brandelyn would have to pay for everything to get her to go back again. A small town Oregonian could as easily throw the shade right back at the city. "Yet you managed to move to the west coast and be perfectly content in a tiny town like this. Who would imagine?"

"Not my family, that's for sure." Brandelyn pushed herself up and turned off the TV. "You know my story. I went to OHSU for med school, stayed in the area for my residency, took up a practice in a small *lesbian* town, and Bob's your uncle."

"Would you have taken up a small town clinic if it weren't full of lesbians, though?"

Brandelyn leaned forward, her pursed lips coming right for Sunny's. Yet she didn't seal the deal. That wasn't Brandy's style. She liked to instigate, but her romantic follow through left a lot to be desired. *Good thing I like those kinds of games.* Sunny loved it when she felt like the badass who did the brunt of the seducing, even if she was well aware it was Brandy's idea.

"I came here because I knew it would change my life." Brandelyn finally let a kiss linger on Sunny's lips. "And it did. I met the love of my life in this tiny little town."

"You could've met someone else in another place."

"Maybe. Why would I want to? This is the kind of life I'm happy to live."

Those were the kind of words that lit up Sunny's heart and made her remember why she loved Brandelyn so much. *Sometimes, I feel like the only person who sees that soft exterior she secretly possesses.* Maybe not so secretly. Wasn't like Brandelyn purposely put people off or acted like a stuck-up city girl displaced to the countryside (that she claimed to actually love.) Sunny accepted that Brandy was a certain way. People were... certain ways, weren't they? There was always room for improvement, but that didn't mean who they were deep in their hearts was a fault. Some people got along. Others didn't. Some environments were ripe for propagating negativity in certain people. Lots of townsfolk thought that about Brandelyn, who was a perfectly good small town doctor, but lacked in the social skills department. But was Sunny that much better? She was more demure in her confidence, had the credibility of being a homegrown resident, and knew what it meant to live in peaceful isolation for most of one's life, but that didn't mean she was inherently better. She read the local social codes better, perhaps, but did that preclude someone like Brandy from ever fitting in?

Honestly, Sunny appreciated someone so different from her. Brandy brought out the voice that was often suppressed deep inside Sunny's body. When a girl grew up in the country, went to a tiny high school, and had a small selection of friends who were away more often than close... it meant she was used to the quiet, including in herself.

Brandelyn's brand of noise was a breath of fresh air.

"Soooo you're staying the night, right?" Sunny asked again. "Don't make me ask a third time. I might decide I'm sleeping solo."

"Like I said, my family…"

"They're gossiping about you right now, anyway. Why not prove them right?" Sunny took her fiancée by the hands and drew her toward the bedroom. Clothes were left unceremoniously behind on the coffee table. The laundry basket was kicked out of the way. Sunny was a woman on a mission to make love to the woman she would soon marry.

Brandy seemed into it, too. Her giggles and the sheepish way she turned her head when she realized what Sunny wanted went against the demeanor of a doctor. *How many women in this town can say they've slept with the doctor? Ooh, not many!* Maybe there were dates Sunny didn't know about, but she didn't care. Brandelyn was all hers, always.

Their kisses were as light as the dust swirling by the window. Their touches were as fervent as the birds singing their songs in the trees. Their little sounds beautifully melded into a place of private serenity.

Sunny held onto this moment. She didn't know when she would get to experience it again, even during their upcoming honeymoon. Because nothing beat the simple bliss of a lazy day at home.

Chapter 9

BRANDELYN

Lest her mother disappoint her, Cathy chastised her daughter for "leaving us all alone in this strange house while you're off having premarital relations. What? You think it's different because it's a woman? I don't care how many babies can get made. It just isn't done. Why are you bringing up Lizzie? This has nothing to do with her boy!" Brandelyn offered no apologies, although she did assure her parents that she would give them more notice if they were left to their own devices for so long again. At least they didn't let Brutus go unwalked or unfed. The boy was getting *fat* with so many people around.

So was Brandy, who blamed PMS, stress, and binge eating when she wasn't paying attention. Her mother's cooking was so full of carbs and fat that Brandelyn was better off eating half and calling it a day. Especially with her dress fitting a week and a half before the wedding.

The final one. *The final one!*

"Please sit still," asked Apple Abernathy, the seamstress who had come recommended based on Yelp! reviews. She tugged on Brandelyn's hem and tightened the waist that pooled around the feet. Every time Brandy's bust was bothered, her breasts heaved toward her chin in unnatural ways. Monica thought it absolutely hilarious that both Brandy *and* Lizzie must suffer for the bridal good. (Lizzie was having none of the spaghetti straps of her baby pink gown messing with her tan. When someone pointed out that her tan was sprayed on, she stormed off to the ladies' room and refused to come out until her mother apologized.)

"How much do you weigh?" Cathy was definitely not apologizing for that. Not even with a Snickers bar in her mouth and her phone constantly pointed to her face. "Really, Brandy, haven't you learned since prom? You always gain ten pounds at this time of year. You should've taken that into account when you bought this dress. Get a size up!"

"First of all." Brandelyn almost lost the rest of her thought after the wind was knocked out of her. Apple apologized and loosened her grip. "I counted my blessings that I could lose enough weight to fit into *this* size." She didn't know when she became a size ten, but she'd be damned if she picked up a twelve for her wedding dress! "Second, I'm bloating from PMS. *You* should've learned that from my eighth grade graduation." She didn't bring up any further details. Like how eighth grade graduation was mired with a giant stain on her skirt by the end of the ceremony. She was the only girl for the class group photo that had a sweatshirt tied around her midsection and tears coming out of her eyes.

"You're really cutting it close having your wedding so close to your period!" Cathy had to shout that for the whole boutique to hear, huh? Lizzie snickered while Monica rolled her eyes. Apple kept her head down and acted like she hadn't heard anything. "You're a doctor! Get yourself one of those pills that makes you skip!"

"You mean *birth control?*"

"Is that what it does?"

Brandelyn didn't have the time or patience to explain how birth control had that effect under certain circumstances. Cathy was a woman who rarely listened to her daughter's doctoral advice, anyway. She was too busy asking websites for subpar information. *That's my whole family. How did I make it out alive? They always think it's cancer!* Like every single patient who walked through the door, but it was more infuriating coming from her own family.

"My period will be over before the wedding," Brandy insisted. "Unless you guys keep stressing me out to the point it's freakin' late!"

Apple offered her squirmy client a weak smile. "There's nothing we can't do about a little bloat, dear. This dress has plenty of give for half an inch or so."

Oh, a whole half an inch!

"Now, *please* sit still. This is delicate work I'm doing back here. I don't want to accidentally screw up the fine beadwork the crafters did."

Brandy took the hint. *If I make her screw it up, I'm being charged to fix it.* Brandelyn had already spent enough money on the dress and these minor alterations. What in the world made her think she had more to spare after all this was over? Thousands of dollars on her credit card. Boom. Done.

She'd be paying it off longer than it took her to pay off her student loans.

"I'm so jealous of Sunny right now," Brandy muttered, hands on her pooching stomach. "It can't be anywhere near as infuriating to bloat in a tux." Not that Sunny ever bloated. She was a solid size eight all year round. Christmas cookies? Size eight. Easter candy? *Eight.* Summer barbecue? That size between six and ten. "I feel like I'm going to explode at any moment. You say there's give back there? Not sure I believe you."

"Oh, Sunny will be so handsome in a tuxedo," Cathy said with a romantic sigh. "She really has the cheekbones for it."

"Doesn't she?" It warmed Brandy's heart to hear it.

"I'm so glad you're having a traditional type wedding, dear. After that city hall mess of Lizzie's, I was afraid neither of my children would have a proper wedding. When you said you were gay and getting married, I knew it was going to be... I dunno. Hippie dresses and period art on the walls."

Everyone turned their heads toward her. Even Apple, who had a pin trapped between her teeth.

"What?" Cathy asked with a shrug. "It happens all the time. I've been to upstate New York, like the rest of you!"

"I can't say I've ever been to a wedding like that, Mom." Brandy huffed. "Not in Eugene or Ashland." Some might guess that Portland was the place for that kind of lesbian wedding. Not so. For the *real* crunchy-catering experience, one went much farther south. Even so, Brandelyn told the truth when she said she had been to lesbian weddings up and down the Willamette and Rogue River Valleys and never saw something like what her mother described. Yet Cathy was a shining example of ignorance when it came to sexualities not her own. She was willing to believe everything and anything she heard, *especially* if it came from a fellow heterosexual. Brandelyn had spent most of her adult life doing two things: medicine, and attempting to unlearn her mother in everything she misunderstood about LGBT issues.

Slowly, but surely...

"Sunny is such a down to Earth girl, though." Cathy shrugged off any minor embarrassment she felt and continued to flip through a bridal magazine left on her chair. "Exactly the kind of person you need in your life, Brandy. Have you met her?" That was directed to the seamstress, still staring down a stitch near Brandelyn's butt.

"Yes, I have had the pleasure."

"I admit, I was really surprised when Brandy told me she was seeing *any* woman, let alone a country girl! Do you know how hard it is to find a genuine country girl where we're from? I mean the ranch types. Not the ones from the hills or the Midwest. They're a dime a dozen lining up for Broadway open-calls."

Brandelyn rolled her eyes. Here her mother went.

"When she moved to Portland to go to medical school, I knew she was going to bring home some Californian beach bum and tell me she was dropping out to become his surfer wife." Lizzie was the only one laughing at that. Everyone else checked their shock and went about their business. Especially Monica, who was glued to her phone. "Instead, she waited twenty years to bring home some sweet girl in boots and flannel. If I had to choose between the two, I would definitely take Sunny!"

"She's definitely something," Lizzie muttered.

"A younger woman, too," Cathy said with a lowered voice, as if her daughter couldn't hear.

"Look at my Brandy, playing that male-dominated field like one of the boys."

"She's thirty-seven!" Brandelyn barked with a sudden jerk of her hips. Apple hissed through clenched teeth as she almost lost her stitch and stabbed Brandy in the ass. "How does that make her a *younger woman?* We were both in our thirties when we started dating." Brandy may be north of forty now, but there was nothing scandalous about the five-year gap between her and Sunny.

"Let your mother have this, please," Cathy drolly said. "She gets so little to be excited about. If I'm happy you're a doctor with a younger spouse..."

Lizzie interrupted, "It gives her something to brag about at the salon. You should hear her, Bran. '*My daughter is such a successful, important doctor that she has a whole practice all to herself in Oregon. She has a thousand patients. She just got engaged to a local and we're going out for the wedding next week! Can you believe her fiancé runs their own business? My daughter is soooo successful! Not like my loser daughter Lizzie! She's a receptionist at a dentist's office instead of being a dentist herself!"*

"That sounds nothing like me," Cathy said with a sniff. "Besides, why shouldn't I brag about my children? You should hear Maria when she goes on about that lawyer son of hers."

"Oh, but Aunt Cathy," Monica said, her sly grin announcing she was about to bring down the mood more than it already was, "what do you say when they ask what *his* name is?"

Brandelyn didn't have to turn around to know that her mother was redder than Apple's name. "Obviously I tell them the name is Sunny!"

"Which they think is *Son*ny..."

"Is it my fault they have preconceptions of west coast country people? Every other man around here is named Sonny, right? Either that or Dirk or Burt or whatever."

Brandy sighed. She didn't expect her mother to be open to her friends about a certain daughter's gayness. *My job is to be the doctor she can brag about to anyone who will listen.* Yet that had come with a small price as well. When Brandelyn announced her intentions to go to medical school, her mother kept calling it "nursing school." Her expectations for Brandy's future were so low that she didn't think her daughter would amount to anything more than a nurse. *Not that there's anything wrong with nurses. God knows I've worked with a thousand of them over the years.* She simply hated the association of *women* and *nursing,* as if it were unheard of to mix things up any other way. *Don't forget when I finally got her to understand I intended to become a doctor! "You're not Asian!" That was it. That was her reaction.* Never mind describing the existence of male nurses...

Cathy continued to flip through her magazine. Did she know that everyone in the room was judging her right now?

"A few more stitches, dear," Apple said to Brandy. "You're doing wonderfully. Should be finished soon, and your dress will be *all* ready for your big day!"

Brandelyn inhaled a deep breath for strength. Right. This was about *her* day. The big day she had been dreaming about since she was a little girl curled up in front of her father's Manhattan TV. *"Daddy, is that what most weddings look like?" "No, Peaches, most are a lot simpler than that one." "Can I have a wedding like that, Daddy?" "If you find the perfect prince charming, I don't see why not."*

Prince charming. Yes. That's what Brandelyn had found when she moved to Paradise Valley and first laid eyes on the lovely Sunny Croker in the nicest dive bar around. She may not have a title, or riches beyond measure, but she had a sweet smile and the kind of quiet kindness that Brandelyn had been searching for ever since she left New York. Easy enough to put that into perspective when her family wasn't around. Now, though?

They'll see exactly what kind of prince charming she is on our wedding day. Brandelyn's favorite way to calm her nerves was to imagine what she would see when she turned the corner on the aisle, arm in arm with her father who was due to arrive in another few days. *I'll turn. I'll see her, my prince charming.* Sunny knew how to clean up when she really put her mind to it. The tux, the hair. Maybe a little makeup, if Sunny felt frisky. Her friend Anita really knew how to style her. Wasn't one of Anita's jobs as Sunny's Best Woman to make sure the bride-groom looked her absolute best for the *bride*-bride?

I am Diana, she is Charles. I am Kate, she is William. Brandelyn wasn't concerned how such royal matches actually ended. She only cared about the picture-perfect scene. The flowers. The sunshine. The people lining up to see the bride and groom in all their glory. Brandy didn't need to marry a man to have a groom. Realizing that her ideal wedding was still in her grasp even if she married a woman had been one of the happiest thoughts of her life. It was second only to meeting Sunny, falling in love, and having her proposal accepted.

It would be the happiest day of Brandy's life. She knew that it would be Sunny's, too.

That was part of the beauty, wasn't it?

Chapter 10

SUNNY

The only way Sunny would get some quality face-to-face time with her fiancée was if she found Brandelyn during working hours. Outside of them? Brandy's time was commandeered by her family, and more and more of them showed up every day. Sunny had been cleaning the guest rooms at Waterlily House when she realized it was time to have a heart-to-heart with the woman she was about to marry. *Soon, my extended family will be here as well. We really won't have any time, then.* Sunny knew that the last thing she should do was spring a giant surprise on her fiancée on their wedding day. They were adults. They were mature. Now was the time to step forward and clear this foggy air.

Too bad Brandelyn had crammed in as many appointments as she could before she went on break.

"Hey, Cici." Sunny wrung her hands as she approached the receptionist's desk in Brandy's office. Cars roared by on Main Street outside the window. Shadows of pedestrians filtered through the blinds that offered a little privacy to those sitting in the waiting room. Decades ago, when this clinic was first founded, it had been convenient for it to be right on Main Street. Now, however, there were calls of concern that convenience had trumped privacy. All of it made Sunny grateful that she didn't live in town. Privacy was a big enough concern between the guests at her B&B, but at least she didn't have to worry about sensitive information breaking out into the open.

Cici the receptionist looked up from her files with a smile. Her wiry silver-black hair and big reading glasses made her look more like a librarian than a receptionist, but she had the kindly demeanor patients requested. Unlike Paradise Valley's only full-time librarian, who was known to make kids cry with one irate look. "Hi, Sunny. Are you looking for Dr. Meyer? She's currently with a patient right now."

"Oh, I figured. I know how busy she is right now."

"Yes, yes, we're totally booked with appointments until she goes off next week. I hear somebody's getting married soon?" Her glossy pink lips expanded into a toothy grin. There was a smidge of that pink gloss on her two front teeth.

"I hear somebody's getting some much-deserved time off soon."

"Dr. Meyer's giving me half-pay for it, too! Can you believe it? I didn't have to ask for it off and she pays me. She must be in a really good mood." That came with a wink.

Sunny had to regain her composure before replying. "I can wait until she has a little time. I was running some errands around town and realized there was something I really need to talk to her about. We don't have much time for private chats before the big day."

"Oh, I've heard alllll about the family taking over her house." That was the sagest nod Sunny had seen all month, and she had wedding-types and high-brow guests alike up her butt. "I can let the doctor know you want to see her, but no guarantees. She's booked until five, and I had to really wiggle that appointment in. Brandy will be staying in a little late tonight as it is."

"I only need ten minutes." Sunny clasped her hands together. She didn't want to say she was *begging,* but she was kinda begging. "It's not life and death, but it's pretty important. Tell her it has to do with the wedding." Hey, it was the truth, although Sunny hated to play with her fiancée's emotions like that.

"I'll see what I can do."

"Thank you." Sunny pulled her phone out of her pocket and sat in the waiting room. Nobody else was there, so she helped herself to some water from the cooler, perused the magazines, and finally sat next to the giant fake orchid arrangement.

She settled on her phone. Good thing, for there were some messages from Dahlia about their upcoming reservation at Waterlily House.

It was the perfect distraction while Sunny waited. There was no obsessing over what she would say or how she should say it. No working herself up into a mental sweat as she anticipated her fiancée's reactions. As long as Sunny stayed focus on her own work, let alone built up her confidence as she handled her business with professionalism, she was convinced that everything would work swimmingly with Brandelyn.

The door to the back rooms opened. Out stepped an elderly man who briefly exchanged glances with Sunny before stopping to talk to Cici about upcoming appointments. Brandelyn, in her white coat, stethoscope, and hair pulled back, stepped out with a clipboard in her hand. She barely saw Sunny since she was so focused on her clipboard.

"Be right with you," she robotically said.

"Brandy." Sunny stood up, already in awe at the sight of her fiancée in such a professional get up. *It kills me every time.* Sunny wouldn't say she was sexually attracted to the look of Dr. Meyer, but she definitely responded with the kind of awe and respect that affected a woman for the rest of her meager existence. *First time I saw her like this... shit, she was my doctor!* Sunny changed insurance and had to go elsewhere long before they started dating, but she could still remember thinking the woman with her dark, curly hair and no-nonsense attitude was one of the hottest women in town. *I was shocked when she asked me out later.* At a bar, no less! Who knew doctors went to bars?

Brandelyn had to double-take in Sunny's direction before she acknowledged her. "Oh, hey," she said. "Give me a moment?"

There was something she had to tell her patient, apparently. Sunny remained sitting, ready to leap up and follow her fiancée into her office at any moment. *Great. Now I'm rehearsing shit in my head.* She fidgeted with her phone. Could this be over with already?

The man stepped outside. Brandelyn motioned for Sunny to follow her into the back.

"I've got about ten minutes to spare before my next appointment needs me."

Sunny didn't need more than ten minutes to break the news to Brandy. *How am I going to do it, though? Gently? Beat around the bush? Be direct?* Direct. Yes. Less time, and like ripping off a Band-Aid. She would have sighed if she thought it would give her any strength.

"What's up?" Brandelyn's demeanor chilled as she shut the door to her office and motioned for Sunny to have a seat with her at the desk. Photos, files, and floral paintings adorned the room Brandy spent most of her working days inhabiting. She may have only worked three or four days a week, but she made the most of it. "If you're here, it must be pretty serious."

"I couldn't text you about it, that's true." Sunny sat down. "I would have normally dropped by after you were done with work, but with your family here..."

"Ugh. Don't remind me. I never thought of this room as my oasis, but it has been ever since Hurricane Meyer arrived from New York." Brandelyn rolled her eyes as she sat down.

"Although it hasn't stopped my mother from trying to barge in on my appointments."

"Yeah, you told me about that."

Brandy waited a few seconds before clearing her throat. "So, what's up?"

Lord, here it came. The moment of truth. The one thing she had been holding back that whole year. "It's about the wedding."

It must have been the way she said it. Perhaps Brandy sensed the panic in Sunny's voice. *Oh, my God! Look at her! She thinks I'm going to call off the wedding!* That couldn't have been farther from the truth. Sunny better rectify this right now before Brandelyn launched into a million words that had nothing to do with what was going on between them.

"I'm not... I don't..." Sunny squeezed her hands into fists and inhaled a deep breath. "I don't want to wear a tux to the wedding," she said upon exhale.

She kept her eyes closed as she awaited Brandelyn's response. Yet all Sunny heard was the tapping of a pen against the desk. Or maybe that was Brandy's foot tapping against the floor.

Something tapped. Sunny's sanity? Her heart, slowly losing its size and luster? *I'm screwed.* Why hadn't Brandelyn said anything yet? Was she so aghast by her fiancée's confession that she was gearing up for a giant explosion?

Sunny finally opened her eyes. Brandelyn looked back at her, a frown accompanying her elbow digging into her desk. It certainly had been a pen smacking against the desk.

"Very funny," Brandy said.

"Huh?"

"I know you like to pull my leg, Sun, but now really isn't the time. My sister had a meltdown at her dress fitting. You should've seen it. It was like she didn't get the memo that cleavage *and* a plunging neckline is like advertising to all of small-town America that you're a giant hussy. My mom called her a slut! God." Brandy rubbed both of her temples. "Sorry. I'm not in the mood for shenanigans right now. I'll get my sense of humor back for the honeymoon."

Sunny sank into her seat. "I'm not pulling your leg. I'm not joking." She bit her lip. "I've been hanging onto a dress for a while now. I was... I was hoping to wear it to the wedding, but I know how much you wanted me in a tux so I, uh... I haven't mentioned it before now."

The silence in Brandy's office almost cracked Sunny in half. Nor could she get a proper reading of her fiancée's expression. Brandy had completely shut down, the words she chewed either made of pure arsenic or sweeter than the kind of sugared honey Sunny's mother once added to sun tea. *It was... not good. But it was meant to be good. God, help me. It's that one, isn't it?* Brandy stewed in everything she wanted to say but didn't have the guts to blurt.

"You're serious?" she finally asked.

Sunny slowly nodded. "I bought the dress before you said I should wear a tux. I don't know why I didn't say anything earlier. Guess I thought you would be..."

Laughter cracked through the room. Brandy slapped her hand on her desk, her grin so wide that it frightened poor Sunny, who continued to sink farther into her chair.

"Holy crap, Sun, you got me good." The laughter continued as Brandy flung herself back into her swivel chair and almost knocked the whole thing over. Figurines rattled on the desk. A paper almost lost its spot on the edge. Sunny's eyes were drawn to the diplomas and certifications hanging above her fiancée's head. "I thought you were serious for a moment. Damn. Can't say I'm mad about it, though. I *really* needed a good laugh recently. Phew."

Sunny didn't know whether to cry or barge out of Brandy's office. *She doesn't believe me? How can she not believe me?* She held one hand against her chest and promised herself that she wouldn't cry. Not in front of Brandy. Not over something as important as this.

"I'm not joking," she said.

It took Brandelyn a few more seconds to finally stop laughing. When she did, it was with confusion swimming in her dark brown eyes. "What?" she asked, humor drained from her face.

Sunny folded her arms, hoping it would propel her posture as she took her stand. "I said I'm not joking. I don't want to wear a tux at our wedding." *Our* wedding. That was the operative word here. Brandy wasn't the only one getting married. Maybe Sunny had a few other things she cared about. There was meeting in the middle and making concessions, but it wasn't up to Sunny to give up what went on her own body. "I've already bought a dress I really like, you know, like you've got a dress, too. I'm letting you know that I'll be wearing it to the wedding."

Brandy remained silent.

"I know it's always been your big vision to wear a big, fluffy princess dress and marry someone wearing a tux... 'cause you love the optics, the aesthetics, whatever... but maybe I don't want to play that role. Maybe I'd like to feel like a princessy girl on my wedding day?"

Brandy gripped her pen in both hands. Was she about to snap it in half? Maybe this was when Sunny should start running. "It's so unlike you to be that kind of woman."

"That *kind* of woman?"

Sunny didn't trust the look on Brandelyn's face. Was she about to snap at her? Cry? Ask why Sunny dared to humiliate her in private like this? Sunny hated how she could only sit there and guess her fiancée's reactions. *I hate that this is a thing.* Standing up for herself and what she wanted at her own damned wedding shouldn't have been this dramatic. How could she marry a woman who didn't respect her wishes? Who said things like, "*It's so unlike you to be that kind of woman,*" when Sunny announced that she wanted to wear a dress?

Brandy softly lowered her pen to her desk. Her posturing was more snotty, big city doctor condescending to her small town patient than one fiancée talking to the other. "I didn't mean it that way," she said, that terse tone striking Sunny right in the heart. "I mean... you have never come across as the kind of woman who wants to wear a dress for *any* occasion."

"Would've been one thing if you let me make that decision, you know. Instead, you basically told me what I would be wearing. How could you assume something like that?"

Brandy gasped.

"I'm sorry." Why was Sunny apologizing? She wasn't the one fighting for her right to pick her own outfit at her own wedding! "It's not fair. You get to have the image you want for your wedding. So, what, because I get a wedding outside of a church, I have to wear whatever you want me to in return?"

"It's not like that. I genuinely thought you would want to wear a..."

"Why? I'm not *that* butch." If the contest were between her and half the women in Paradise Valley, she definitely lost the competition. Sunny was positively *femme* compared to the likes of the sheriff and certain EMTs screeching down Main Street on a bad day. Not that Sunny put much stock in those representations. She simply wore what she liked, styled her hair a certain way, and didn't give a shit if a well-meaning guest mistook her for a young man. Words like "butch" and "femme" had their place in Paradise Valley, but to Sunny Croker, she was content to do her thing and hope nobody gave her crap for it.

She never thought that a woman she might soon marry would be at the top of the crap-slinging list. But Brandy loved her traditional roles. She loved tradition, period. Even the wedding had to be a certain way to cater to that old school vision Brandy had been brought up with and never thought to change. Aspects of it were attractive, honestly. While Brandelyn was egalitarian in terms of who paid for what – and for God's sake, *she* was the one who popped the question – she very much believed in one of them being the firm, steady provider and the other a more homemaking type. The irony came when self-proclaimed femme Brandy was the provider and sometimes-called-soft-butch Sunny the one into gardening, cooking, and housekeeping. Was it different because Sunny still ran her own business and always had her hands dirty? Or was it different because she fulfilled Brandy's fantasy of the rural rube who might not have the best education, but had the respect of everyone in town because they were a good person?

Honestly, Brandelyn couldn't follow her own rules, so she could piss off.

"Apparently, I've made an error of judgment." Brandy wouldn't look Sunny in the eye. Did that mean she truly conceded her attitude? Or that she didn't find Sunny *worth* looking in the eye? "I had been making plans based on what I assumed *you* would want. Besides, you put most of the wedding planning in my hands. Or do you remember absolving yourself of those responsibilities?"

"Only because it was like having too many cooks in the kitchen!" Sunny rethought that. "More like too many cooks in *your* kitchen. I always hate trying to bring a little bit of myself into this wedding. I might step on your toes, or ruin your childhood vision, or whatever is the issue with me wanting to get married at the house or wear a dress. I bet if I asked if we had fewer orchids at the wedding, you'd die."

"Why do you have to come for the orchids like that?"

"See? That's what I'm talking about. Look, Bran, I don't care if the wedding colors are pink or purple or blue or whatever. I don't care if you want a whole bouquet of sunflowers. We could have vegan lasagna served with a side of rainbow sprinkle cake. You want to throw real rice instead of birdseed? Be my guest. Let's watch those birdie bellies explode."

"What are you going *on* about?"

But Sunny wouldn't let up. Not when she looked her fiancée right in the eye and said, "How do I know that the only reason you're marrying me *isn't* because I check your boxes and nothing more? What if I grew out my hair and started wearing skirts for here on out? Would you still love me?"

Brandy's jaw fell. "Where is all of this coming from? Have I ever treated you as someone less than human? Because that's what you're making me sound like right now."

Honestly? Sunny didn't know. She had worked herself up into such a frenzy that she second-guessed everything she thought and knew about her relationship. What if it *was* true that Brandy loved her, not for who she was inside, but how she looked on the outside? Because Sunny completed her precious aesthetic? What if she was willing to call off the wedding the moment Sunny walked down the aisle in a dress? Right now, the plan was for her to play the freakin' groom in her little tux and without her mom or dad to give her away. *I'm supposed to stand up there with Anita and look pleased as punch to have my impending wife coming at me.*

Sunny stood up, making sure she still had her phone before she walked out of Brandy's office. She'd be damned if she stayed around any longer and made a bigger fool of herself. Brandelyn had helped her plenty with that so far.

Chapter 11

BRANDELYN

"Can you believe that?" Brandy scoffed over her glass of red wine at dinner. While her stepfather grilled on the patio, Brandelyn sat with the women in her family, drinking wine, snacking on fresh grapes a patient delivered earlier that day, and going over the strange altercation Brandy and Sunny had a few hours ago. "She says all this stuff out of nowhere and runs away! She won't respond to my texts or calls." Brandelyn was "this" close to driving over to Waterlily House and confronting Sunny, but she knew that would be a terrible idea. When Sunny was ready to apologize, she'd contact her fiancée.

"Sounds like cold feet to me." Cathy motioned for one of her daughters to refill her wine glass. Smoke from the charcoal heating up the grill rolled across the patio with the next breeze. Brandelyn's stepfather waved his hand and grinned when his grandsons laughed. The boys went back to tossing a ball around Brandy's backyard. Brandy tipped the bottle of wine into her mother's glass and shook her head. "What?" Cathy continued. "She's making up stuff to whine about, isn't she? Starting a fuss for no reason other than to break off the wedding."

Brandy almost choked on her wine. "Break off the wedding? She's having a little snit. I highly doubt she's going to call anything off."

"I didn't say she would. I said she's getting cold feet. Everyone does it, dear! Don't you remember how Lizzie was at city hall when she got married?"

"Why do you have to drag me into this?" Lizzie snapped.

"Because I remember you crying in the women's restroom on the fourth floor! *Baaw, baaaaw, I don't wanna marry the man who knocked me up although literally the only reason I'm pregnant was so he would finally marry me!"*

Lizzie turned around in her seat with a scoff. "I was hormonal, all right? Matt absolutely creamed my hormones that first time I was pregnant." Her oldest boy now tackled his brother, the two of them screaming in boyish delight. A neighbor peered over the fence before going back to minding his business. "You can't blame me for that. Or are you trying to imply that Brandy's lady is in a family way?"

"Elizabeth Meyer, you watch your mouth," Cathy said with a huff. "Don't go spreading things like that in a town like this."

The thought of Sunny cheating on me with a guy is so outrageous. "This isn't about any of that, okay? She's accusing me of being a Bridezilla and telling her who to be. You don't do that in lesbian relationships. Not that I expect any of you to understand that."

They merely nodded, as if to say, *"Naturally, we know nothing about it."*

"We women are delicate creatures, no matter who you pair yourself up with." Cathy tipped back her wineglass while her daughters and niece waited for her to complete that thought. Knowing Catherine Meyer, it would either end with a poignant expression, or explode in offense. "Weddings are a big deal. I don't care if you grew up in a cave off the grid and know nothing of traditional customs, you care about your wedding day."

Is she judging me? Brandy honestly couldn't tell. Sometimes, her mother was such a master of passive-aggression that she put most of these Oregonians to shame. She often attributed Cathy's mannerisms to *motherhood, incarnate.* Particularly a mother of grown women who kept dragging their drama out into the open. *Not that you would know anything about that, right, Mom?* Brandy could remember those Halcyon days of catching her grandmother scolding Cathy for this and that. Sometimes in public, usually in the middle of their home kitchen. Grandma was dead now, but if Brandelyn closed her eyes and imagined that old woman with blush caked on her face and plastic jewelry hanging from her wrists, she heard the berating tone.

"What are you trying to say?" Brandelyn finally cast her bait, hoping Cathy would bite.

She merely hoped she didn't catch a wallop of a judgmental fish.

"You keep saying that Sunny put the wedding planning 'into your hands.'" Cathy shook her head. "You make it sound like she wants no say, or that you two have *such* syncretic tastes that you could vote to get married by a man in a purple rabbit suit and Sunny would think it the coolest thing since the Model-T. Also, I wouldn't believe you. Because for a woman to give up that much control of her own wedding, it means one of two things."

Brandy didn't ask what those were. Her mother would be happy to inform her.

"Either she's a spineless toboggan who can't stand up for what she wants..."

Lizzie leaped in to finish the thought. "Or you're such a monster about it that it ain't worth it, sis."

Brandelyn slammed her half-empty wineglass on the table. A few yards away, her stepfather declared the burgers almost ready. Did anyone have those plates of veggies for him to throw on next? Anyone? Kids? *Grand*kids?

"I'm not a monster," Brandy said, ignoring her stepfather alongside everyone else. "I would greatly appreciate it if you all didn't run around declaring me a Bridezilla, either. I've got enough problems with my fiancée acting like I am one."

"Because it's not like enough people saying it's true actually makes it true, right?" Lizzie asked with a scoff. "You're something else, sis."

"What are you talking about?"

The way Brandy barked that nearly brought the backyard to a standstill. Her stepfather looked up from the grill, eyes blinking away the smoke. Her nephews and youngest cousin halted their roughhousing and looked like they were about to be chastised for playing too much. Even the nosy neighbor scurried back down his fence and acted as if he weren't listening in on Brandelyn's drama.

"Look, Bran, we didn't wanna say it..." Cathy uncrossed her legs and leaned forward. For her to abandon her favorite relaxation pose, she was serious about what she was about to say. "You *are* being difficult. I didn't know that your fiancée wearing a suit was your idea."

"How could it not be her idea?" Brandelyn's defensive nature sprang up as if it had been summoned by pentagram and a few choice words in Latin. *A relative for every judgmental point of the star!* Even Brutus's little tail shook as if he prepared for a fight against a summoned demon. "You don't know her as well as I do," Brandy continued. "That is *very* Sunny. I've only seen her wear a skirt like three times since I've known her. The thought of her wanting to wear a dress is absolutely preposterous."

"Gee, a woman wanting to wear a dress at her wedding is *preposterous*." That was Monica's contribution to the conversation. "What will they come up with next?"

"You guys seriously don't get it!" How could Brandy get them to understand the Sunny that she knew? How was she expected to wade through the semi-offensive comments born of ignorance? "Lots of women wear suits to their weddings around here. It's not a big deal."

"Apparently, it is to *your* woman," Cathy chided.

Brandelyn looked at the people staring her down like she was an unholy mess. Really? They were doing this? All Brandy cared about was having a nice wedding. Why couldn't her mother see that she truly had everyone's best interests in mind? *She makes it sound like I'm pushing some selfish agenda on everyone!* Shouldn't her mother be happy that Brandy held the reins on this wedding? She said so herself that she was grateful that Brandy was having a "traditional" wedding. Why weren't they on the same page?

"Look," Cathy recoiled from the look on her daughter's face, "it might be time for you to step back from the wedding planning and check in with your fiancée. She grew a damn spine and tried to put her foot down about something. That's when you have to listen. If you can't listen to her now, then what good is it going to be when you're married, she's screaming, and you're pretending you don't hear anything?"

"She *has* put her foot down about things," Brandy mumbled. "Why do you think we're getting married at her house instead of in the church?" She honestly expected her semi-religious family to be aghast that no church weddings were on the docket. Then again, after Lizzie's city hall affair...

"This sounds much more personal than a church vs. home wedding," Monica said with a snort. "The woman doesn't want to wear a suit. Who are you to tell her that she has to?"

"That's *not* the issue!" Brandelyn slapped both hands down on the table. "I would never tell her what to wear!"

"Okay, but, like..." Here came that tone Lizzie loved when she got to hold something over her big sister. "It doesn't sound like you're holding a gun to her head, Bran. Sounds like you're making her mad with the assumptions."

"You don't take criticism well, so..." Monica continued.

"What does criticism have to do with it?"

Seriously, what was this *really* about? Everyone danced around some truth they were so afraid to tell Brandelyn, as if she were going to explode from the *bad* criticism she apparently couldn't take. *This is ridiculous. Since when is everyone ganging up on me? I don't have time for this.* Her wedding was a week and a half away. It was too late to make major changes, anyway. Why was everyone prancing about on their tip toes? Did they really think Brandy was a "Bridezilla?" Brandelyn the Bridezilla. It had a ring to it, didn't it?

Her stepfather brought over a plate of cooked hamburgers. As if he were about to get yelled at for daring to encroach on sacred, feminine space, he gingerly placed the plate in the center of the table, careful to avoid the glasses and bottle of wine. "Anyone figure out where those buns are yet?" he whispered.

"I'm not a Bridezilla," Brandy muttered, elbows on the table and hands fisting her hair.

"There's a bag of buns on the counter," Cathy told her husband. "Don't mind my daughter.

She's grumpy because she doesn't take criticism well."

"I'm *not* a Bridezilla."

"That's right," Lizzie said. "If you keep telling yourself that, it will come true."

"You guys suck."

Monica snorted. "Go ahead and take your whining out on us, hun. That way when it comes time to make nice with your lady, you can have a clear head."

Brandy blushed. In all this talk of how defensive Brandy was, she had forgotten to remind herself that *she* wasn't the center of the controversy. It was Sunny, who had kept a secret from Brandy for so long because she was afraid of her fiancée's reaction. *What kind of fiancée am I, anyway? She doesn't feel comfortable telling me what she really wants.* Then again, Brandelyn had never encountered something like this before. Not in her years with Sunny, anyway. The lovely, energetic, amiable Sunny.

Here I was, stomping my foot all over her. No wonder Sunny had to grow a backbone.

Chapter 12

SUNNY

The thing about having a bachelorette party at a dive bar? It didn't matter how few people Sunny invited along. Eventually, the whole town was in on it.

Especially at the lesbian dive, which was full of locals and out-of-towners alike.

"This girl over here is getting married!" Anita snapped a party hat that said *BRIDE* onto Sunny's head and led her through the depths of Paradise Lost, the only bar in town that catered to the overwhelming clientele. The other bar, Wolf's Hill Dive, was usually Sunny's preference when it came to the food and drink, but it wasn't the kind of place to parade one's gay wedding through like it was Pride. (Not that she couldn't, per se. The fine folks at Wolf's Hill Dive were firm supporters of all the gays about town. They simply had more men than women most of the time.)

Cheers erupted. The women enjoying their end-of-the-week drinks and date nights with their gals turned around to lift their beers and spirits. Most of them probably recognized Sunny, one of the two stars of that month's biggest wedding. *Shit, they're all invited, I bet.* Sunny had handed over her list of fifty people she'd like to see invited and allowed Brandelyn to take care of the rest. How that list of fifty people ballooned to three hundred would always be beyond Sunny, who thought they had overlapping friends, concluded that Brandy wanted a proper audience, and that was all there was to it.

"This gal right here," Anita continued, her own party hat askew as more women gathered around them on the stage, "is marrying the woman who you talk to about your itchy crotches, so you better buy her a freakin' drink!"

Usually, the erupting laughter would have amused Sunny, who took most things with the kind of good humor that won her more friends than enemies. But ever since she rushed out of the clinic, tears streaming down her cheeks, she hadn't the heart to think about the wedding. She hadn't exchanged a word with her fiancée, although not for a lack of trying on Brandy's part. *I barely missed her when she finally drove up to Waterlily House to corner me.* That was the day Sunny drove to PDX to pick up her aunt and uncle from the airport.

That aunt was *really* tickled about being in a gay bar on a Saturday night.

"Oh my *God,* look at this!" Jill pulled her plastic straw out of her cocktail and waved around the loops that looked like boobs. "Every bachelorette party I've been to has been an utter dick-fest. This one's going down in the history books, and it's barely started!"

That was the plan, anyway. Plenty of gratuitous mammaries in Sunny's face, every vagina joke under the sun, and an array of games, drinks, and gifts that reminded everyone in the room that they were never too young to understand the meaning of the word "carpet" when uttered in a gay bar.

It only got crazier as the drinks filled everyone's veins.

"Open it!" someone barked from the side of the stage, where Sunny and Anita sat with a stack of gifts by their side. "It's in an Amazon box, so you know it's raunchy!"

Sunny grabbed her beer for another drink of courage. She dove for the scissors that had aided her in the opening of other presents, but her shaking hands and falling torso told Anita to leap in and intervene. Good thing Anita had stayed mostly sober that evening.

"Let me get that for you, Sun." Anita left Sunny propped up on her side on the floor and popped open the box. "Oh... oh my God, who can fit this in their hooha?"

Aunt Jill was the first to shove aside everyone in her line of sight. "Whoa!" she exclaimed, tossing her drink into the air. Red liquid landed on another woman's head. That woman didn't look like she had noticed. "Now that's what I'm talking about! That's some wedding night shit right there, Sunny!"

Her sister, Sunny's mother, perked up from her conversation in the corner and died of embarrassment when she saw the behemoth toy. *This is not my first time holding a dildo in the same room as my mother.* Sunny was too tipsy to remember the last time, but she was pretty sure it was when she and her mother stumbled into a Spencer's Gifts.

Aunt Jill remained front and center at the stage like she was at her favorite rock concert. Someone refilled her spilled drink and cheered her on for being a supportive family member. Her two thumbs up and giant smile reminded Sunny why she had protested the presence of family at her bachelorette party.

Didn't help that she felt like *shit*. The alcohol was supposed to take the apprehension off her mind. Instead, it made her fixate on what she was doing. Namely, preparing to marry Dr. Brandelyn Meyer sometime the next week.

Sunny overturned a small plastic bag and unearthed a dozen glow-in-the-dark pencil toppers shaped like breasts. She held a neon green one up to the stage light above her and said, much more loudly than she intended, "These will be the biggest tits in my marriage."

More laughter erupted. Anita gently pointed out that Sunny had perfectly sizable breasts.

To that, Sunny could only reply, "You would know. You stared at them in the locker room during high school."

The laughter soon turned into gasps of scandalized awe. The only woman in the room who wasn't laughing was Anita, who checked her blushing, looked to her partner in the audience, and said, "Nobody stared at boobs like you did, Sun. Let me guess. The whole reason you went out with Brandelyn was because you liked how she stacked that white coat."

Sunny wasn't surprised to hear some inappropriate murmurs from the audience. Everyone had an opinion about the kind of sexy doctor fantasies Brandelyn served. Even those who didn't otherwise find her attractive had to admit she had "the demeanor down."

"Truth or dare," Anita said to her best friend.

Sunny, guzzling more beer like it was going out of style, foolishly said, "Truth!"

Everyone leaned in to listen to Anita's question. "You ever have a bit of roleplay with everyone's favorite town doctor? Come on. Her patients are dying to know."

For every person wrinkling their nose in disdain, there was another waggling her eyebrows as if this were the question they had been waiting for all night. Sunny pulled herself back up into the chair in the center of the stage, the one bedecked in pink streamers and purple glitter. Anita had really dug into her old school supplies for this party. *How much did the owner of this joint threaten her when she brought out the glitter, though?*

"All I'll say," Sunny interspersed her sentence with a burp, "is that she really knows how to snap those latex gloves onto her hand."

Sunny couldn't tell if the crowd's reaction was from how funny they found that... or... well, she didn't want to know. *The most roleplaying Brandy and I ever do is when she gets on top for two seconds.* One would think Brandelyn was allergic to riding the waves, so to speak. *Every time she ends up on top of me, you'd think it was an accident. "Whoops! How did I get up here?"* Sunny could practically hear that in Brandy's voice. *"I don't belong up here! I wear dresses!"*

The usual assortment of bachelorette party games appeared. *Pin the Nipples on the Playboy Bunny* was a staple in Paradise Lost, even without a good reason to play. A wedding bell-shaped pinata full of red jellybeans spilled on top of Sunny's head when Aunt Jill gave it a mighty whack with an old baseball bat. The drunker people became, the more they uproariously laughed at the off-colored jokes and gifts popping out of boxes left and right. Everything happened as sober Sunny would have wanted. People split off into groups, laughing over the old times, their own relationships, and who they wanted to bone. Drunk and hurt Sunny, however, wasn't satisfied. She demanded a sacrifice, and it had to come at her own expense.

Because it wasn't fair. How could these people prance around the bar, cheering her relationship to *Dr. Brandelyn Meyer,* and make it sound like a good thing? Didn't they know the real Brandy? What? Did they think that because they went home going, *"That doctor sure is a good doctor. I wonder if she acts that uptight all the time..."* they were somehow wrong? Did they want to believe that people were that much different than from who they were at their jobs? Was Lorri Abrams gonna sit there at the bar and pretend that she wasn't Little Miss Black Humor at the hardware store *and* at home with her partner? Or was Mikaiya Marcott, who famously made her living with a Bluetooth in her ear and a MacBook in front of her, bound to declare that she wasn't the prissiest person to ever leave Paradise Valley? Sunny was the first to admit she was exactly the same here in this bar as she was at Waterlily House. *I'm a fucking ray of sunshine, after all! Ask my mother over there!* Her mother, who was only there out of support for her daughter, would rather not talk about gender and sexuality. She was content to sit with some older friends and nurse their gin and tonics.

She should probably clamp her hands over her ears for this.

"Do you guys wanna know what it's *really* like being with big ol' Doctor Meyer?" Sunny went to finish her fifth beer, only to realize *someone* had drunk it for her. *Whoever the bitch is, I'ma cut her.* The irony? She scraped her arm against her chair two seconds later. "Because I can give you the freakin' tell-all right here."

She stumbled from her chair to the edge of the stage. It was only a foot and a half off the ground, which was mediocre for a live stage in a crowded bar, but a lifesaver for a drunk woman named Sunny Croker. Anita and her partner, Bonnie, both leaped forward to catch Sunny in case she fell. *Look at them. They've got panic on their faces. They think I'm gonna splat!* Sunny had perfect control of her motor skills, thank you very much. She only had two beers!

(It was two, right? Because she only remembered two.) If anyone should be worried about falling over, it should be Aunt Jill. There were three of her. Any one of them could collapse at any moment!

"I'll tell you," Sunny reiterated, already forgetting that she said the same thing a few seconds earlier. *I've only had seven beers tonight. One is hardly anything! I've only had four beers tonight. It's my bachelorette party! I'll have five beers if I want five beers.* Ah, there it was. The correct number. "If you've ever, *ever* had her reach up your blouse with her stethoscope, then you know what it's like." She paused for effect. "Cold, hard, and it's over in five seconds."

The awkward sputtering and chuckles around them had Anita gritting her teeth in disbelief. "Sunny!" she hissed from the front of the stage. "What are you doing?"

"You ever dated a wet fish?" Sunny had to laugh at her choice of words. Wet! Fish! One would think she said that on purpose. "Because I'm gonna marry one. A wet fish who thinks the whole world revolves around her aaaaand she's gonna tell me what to do for the rest of our lives."

The crowd wasn't laughing anymore. Anita, however, was climbing back onto the stage to grab Sunny and go.

"When you come to my wedding next week," Sunny crowed, "I hope you enjoy the surprise of what's going on as much as I do! I don't know what I'm wearing yet! Still waiting for Brandy to get back to me on that!"

Sunny was so plastered that it only took Anita four attempts to drag her into the women's restroom, where she shooed away two loiterers and splashed some cold water onto the bride's face.

"Hey!" Sunny spat the water all over herself. "Whatchu doing that for?"

"I'm trying to get some sense into you, idiot." When Sunny's eyes focused again, she beheld a woman with her arms akimbo and a Serious Teacher Face looking back at her. "You're out there shitting on your fiancée in front of everyone! At your bachelorette party!"

"Huh? I didn't say anything." Sunny rocked back and forth on her feet. Eventually, she braced herself against the chipped bathroom sink. "What are you talking about? I said what everyone is already thinking about *Brandy*." She spat her fiancée's name as if it were verboten. "She's a controlling butthead who has to have everything her way. All the way down to how we have sex. Do you know what happened the last time we had some time to ourselves?" Sunny could clearly remember it, with or without inebriation. *That beautiful, sunshine-filled day in my little cottage at Waterlily House. I threw down my laundry, guided her into my room, annnnnndddd did the same thing we always freakin' do.* "I didn't even come, but she got to like three times before taking a shower."

Eyes rolling and hands turning on the sink, Anita was now compelled to splash some water onto her *own* face. "Thanks for that lovely image, Sun. You know how much I love fantasizing about the same mediocre sex you and the rest of us are having."

"She's gotta feel like a princess at all times, and I've gotta be her prince *charming*. Which means she's a pillow-biting princess who can't get enough of ignoring what *I* want."

"Look, Sun, I know this is really about the wedding." Oh, Anita knew all about what happened in Brandy's office. She was the first person Sunny told after it happened. "I'm sorry things are going rough with her right now, but airing out your dirty laundry at your *bachelorette party* is really not the way to handle it. This is going to bite you in the ass."

"What do you know? You're not the one who is sitting off to the side like a piece of discarded chicken." Sunny spat that, not knowing what the hell *she* was talking about. "I don't want a big ol' wedding, you know? Three hundred people! Who around here has three hundred people to invite to their wedding? The mayor? I don't... I don't *know* three hundred people. Who's coming to my wedding? What are we eating? Who's carrying the rings? I don't know anymore! I feel like I'm going to someone else's wedding!"

"To be fair, Sun, you washed your hands of most of it."

The tears Sunny had been holding back poured from the corners of her eyes. "I wish I haaaaad*n't!*"

Anita lightly patted her friend's shoulder as Sunny ugly-drunken-cried into a large mass of paper towels. *Why do I have to be such a pushover? Why do I always have to be the one to compromise?* That point was only further exacerbated when Brandelyn pointed out the church thing. So what! She still got everything else! She got a lemon cake when Sunny vastly preferred chocolate, to the point she joked about having her own cake at the wedding. Brandy picked a photographer who had albums full of highly Photoshopped images of other people's weddings, and Sunny worried she wouldn't recognize herself in her own wedding photos. *Don't get me started on the flowers!* She knew Brandy wouldn't rest unless there was an orchid garden at the wedding, but did it have to happen at the expense of the flowers Sunny and her aunt had planted over the decades? Some of those bushes had been around since Carter was in office. The wedding planner asked if they could be "relocated" to make room for more seating, and Sunny had to inform both the planner *and* Brandy that there would be no disturbance of the flowers.

And if Brandelyn thought her Pomeranian would be carrying the rings...

If there was one thing Brandy excelled at, it was seducing women and then getting the *hell* under their skin.

"Come here." Anita drew Sunny into an embrace. There they stood, swaying back and forth in a dive bar restroom while Sunny sobbed and Anita adopted her everyday schoolteacher's voice. "I know it's been really stressful and hard. Brandy's been a bit of a... yeah... but you know she loves you, right? I can't imagine there's anyone in this world who can love her like you do, either. This wedding is merely one day in your whole life together. I hate to say it, but most people won't remember it a year from now, but they might remember what you were saying about your love life."

Sunny was still too drunk to feel proper shame for what she had said a few minutes ago. Did she have regrets, though? A few. In the heat of her frustrations, she had implied that Brandelyn was an awful lover. If that wasn't bad enough, she had done it to a number of her fiancée's *patients*. People who would soon go to see her for their ailments and not be able to think of anything beyond, "*Dr. Wet Fish.*"

"Let's clean you up a bit and get you back out there. You're not gonna remember tonight because you're so drunk, but I'll make sure you're having fun at your party, not drunk and crying in the damned bathroom. Let's go."

Sunny felt a little better after she splashed some water on her face and straightened out her clothing. Laughter and music filtered through the door, implying the bar patrons – and Sunny's guests – had already moved on to other topics and games. Although she stumbled through the door, Sunny adopted the attitude that this would be the most fun she had without Brandelyn in a long while, but maybe she'd drink water or Coke for the rest of the night.

The bar fell into silence about five seconds after Sunny emerged from the restroom.

"Oh, that's not good." Anita, who still had her arm wrapped around her friend, said. "Someone's stolen your thunder at your bachelorette party."

"Is it that celebrity lady?" Sunny leaned against the nearest table, nausea overwhelming her again. "Because you have to make a reservation to stay at Waterlily House. She hasn't... she hasn't made a reser... reserva... "

"Nope. It's definitely not that actress," Anita said, staring ahead.

"Did you know that Brandy's sister got married at a New York City courthouse? City hall? Something like that? Her mom was *soooo* pissed."

"Nope," Anita said again. "It's not the mayor."

"Who is..."

The answer came with the parting of the crowd before them. Sunny had to rub her eyes before making out the familiar figure barging through the door and looking around. For her.

Chapter 13

BRANDELYN

While this was certainly unconventional, Brandelyn couldn't help but leave her family behind at the house and drive down to Paradise Lost, the place where she first beheld the beauty she was destined to marry.

Sunny didn't look quite as beautiful now, however. *What the hell happened to her? She's beyond drunk!* Drunk and related to the town crypt keeper, apparently. Poor Sunny looked like she had been smacked with the ugly stick, that carried with it poor posture, sweaty brows, slovenly clothing, and an agape mouth that didn't know how to close. Her usually put together fiancée had left her comb at home, and her eyes were so puffy that Brandelyn had flashbacks to her hay fever patients that usually descended around that time of year.

"What in the..." Brandy was aware that everyone was staring at her. Well, yes. This was her fiancée's bachelorette party, and Brandy was *not* supposed to impose. Yet when she decided to find Sunny and properly apologize for how things had been going in the lead up to their wedding, she knew she couldn't wait. This fissure could no longer divide them. Not in such pivotal days. What if this week foretold the rest of their marriage? It had to be done now. Apologies laid out. A small heart to heart before Sunny got back to her partying. Surely, it wasn't so late that Sunny was on her ass, yes?

Apparently, it was.

"Oh, my God. Is she okay?" Brandy asked Anita, the woman supposedly responsible for this mess. *I'm not one to tell Sunny who to be friends with, but if it weren't for Anita's job as a teacher, I would seriously question her responsible nature.* Like if she had one. Because although Anita dressed herself like a sensible woman, she was usually behind Sunny's party days. Not to mention some of Sunny's wilder ideas...

"She's a little drunk. Someone's been enjoying her bachelorette party, that's all." Anita platonically ran her fingers through Sunny's tangled hair, like a mother attempting to gussy up her unruly child. *I can smell the stench of beer from here. How many did she have?* Sunny could drink more than most assumed from looking at her. Brandy always considered herself a "medium weight," thanks to a healthy dose of wine every day at dinner. When Sunny got to drinking, though? She reminded Brandy that some people could knock back three beers in a row and barely be tipsy. It wasn't until she met the Crokers that she understood.

Seeing Sunny like this? She must have drunk half the stock in Paradise Lost!

"Brandy?" Did Sunny only now realize that her fiancée was here? Why were people staring at them like this? *I have no idea what's going on, and I don't like it.* One thing for people to gossip about Brandy crashing the bachelorette party. Quite another for them to assume the worst. "What... what are you doing here?"

Brandelyn squared her shoulders. "Can we talk in private for a few minutes? There's something I really want to say."

Anita looked between her drunken friend and the woman coming to abscond her. "I mean, sure," Anita said, "but she's pretty sloshed. She also might have... um..."

A middle-aged woman with dyed orange hair and a blue sweater that screamed *I bought this in the city,* rushed up to them with a giant smile on her face. "Hi, Brandy! Remember me? It's Jill, Sunny's aunt!"

Brandy was only slightly taken aback at this woman's sudden presence. "I'm sorry. I don't mean to intrude upon the festivities, but there's something I really need to talk to my fiancée about."

Both Jill and Anita looked to Sunny, who swayed in place and raised her eyebrows as if Brandy came to flirt.

"She's a bit inebriated, don't you think?" Jill

popped a gummy candy into her mouth. Brandy couldn't help but notice that it was shaped like a pair of breasts. *God help me if this is what my bachelorette party is like.* Sunny could have all the inappropriate fun she wanted, as long as she kept her hands to herself, but it really *wasn't* Brandelyn's style. Instead of saying it was nature, however, she chalked it up to years of medical practice. After a while, it was hard to get excited about disembodied breasts.

"Obviously, I can talk to her later, but I didn't think she would be quite like this yet."

"I'm right here, you know." Sunny stood up straight, pulled up her sagging jeans, and did her best impression of *Sober Sunny.* "You wanna talk? All right. Let's go talk outside. I need some fresh air, anyway." She turned to Anita before putting one foot forward. "Could you grab me something to drink? *Not* beer."

"You want a Coke? They got the new ones with orange in them."

"Have her put it on my tab."

Brandy led the way outside, where the cool night air greeted them. She had originally intended to take Sunny to the side of the building for their heart to heart, but she didn't trust Sunny to not fall down the steps – or the handicap ramp, for that matter. So they stood to the side of the entrance, at the top of the ramp where Brandy hoped nobody would disturb them.

"My God, Sun." Brandy pinched her nose. "You reek."

"It's a *party*. You know, people making merry and not giving a shit about pit stank."

Based on the *other* kind of clouds wafting through the parking lot, Brandelyn had a feeling that booze wasn't the only substance people partook in that night. While recent legalization laws made it easier for her to recommend marijuana to her patients, it meant Brandelyn suffered the smell every time she stepped outside. *My nosy neighbors are the worst offenders*. Their perpetual pot cloud kept Brandy coughing every time she went out to water her flowers in the evening.

"My family is making plenty merry in my house right now. My mother discovered my wine stash, for crying out loud, and my stepfather got his sports app working on my TV. I haven't had a damned thought to myself since they got here. Don't get me started on the boys." When they weren't hounding the internet connection playing games on their phones, they were squealing in the yard or raising hell in the street. What noise pollution they didn't contribute with their constant yelling was provided by honking cars. "Look, honey, I didn't plan on coming by and interrupting your party at all tonight. But I don't want us going into the next week on the wrong foot. I... I want to apologize. For everything."

Sunny sobered up faster than Brandy had ever seen before. Was that all it took? Or was the inebriation an excuse for her to act like she had? "Apologize? I don't expect any apologies."

"I want to apologize. I've been a real tyrant in the wedding planning. Especially since... well, I know it's your wedding, too."

Sunny didn't say anything. Was that her way of agreeing that Brandelyn had been an ass? Let alone the last few weeks of insanity!

"I guess I got all caught up in it because, in my mind, I was the bride, you know? I've always want to be a 'bride,' and it didn't matter if I was in a lesbian relationship. I grew up with these notions that the bride is the only one who cares about things. The groom shows up to get it over with and then goes drinking with their buddies. Then we go off on our honeymoon, boom, the fantasy is over. Back to real life." Brandelyn sighed. "When you first told me that you didn't care about the planning as much, I took that as my sign to be the big bride. When you told me I could do most of the planning because it stressed you out too much, I... I went overboard, I know. But I really crossed a line with the dress thing. I'm sorry I reacted the way I did the other day. You honestly surprised me. I swear I wasn't trying to judge you or anything. I... you know I don't like curve balls in my life."

Sunny managed a sloppy smile that gave Brandelyn hope this would soon be behind them. "I'm like a big curve ball, though!"

"Sometimes, yeah." Brandelyn didn't mention that being a "big curve ball" meant they weren't too compatible. Sunny was the right mix of spontaneity and reliability, though. She was as reliable as Brandy needed, while bringing that huge dose of much-needed spontaneity. *Because I'm not doing it for myself, that's for sure.* "That's what I like about you, though. You keep life from being boring. You always keep me guessing."

"Yeah, I... I do stuff like that sometimes..." Sunny scratched the top of her head like she had something to hide. *It's okay, hon, I forgive you for being roaring drunk at your party.* Not that anyone had asked for Brandy's forgiveness. *I love doling it out, though.* She was somewhat inspired by these festivities. Perhaps she might go home and join her family in the raiding of the wine cellar.

"You can wear whatever you want." Brandy took her fiancée's hand and gave it a tight squeeze. "Suit, dress... well, keep it formal, I suppose. If I'm walking down the aisle with an expensive dress to die for, it's only fair that you keep up with me. In fact, your Bridezilla commands it."

Sunny grinned. "You mean that? Because, you know, maybe I'll wear the tux to the ceremony and change into the dress for the reception! Wouldn't that be a good compromise?"

Brandelyn had to admit it played right into the most important aspect of her plans. *The optics of her tux and my dress as we stand at the altar is everything I wanted.* The photographers would be locked and ready to go as they said their cherished vows and exchanged rings. Sunny could spring into the reception wearing boxer shorts and a tank top and Brandy wouldn't give a shit. As long as she was gorgeous for the ceremonial photos!

"No..." she eventually said. "You should only do that if it's what you want. I want you to *feel* as good as you look when we get married, baby." Brandelyn Meyer was not a "baby" person. That word only naturally came out when she was really in the mood, and looking into Sunny's drunken doe-eyes brought out the babies. "I want us riding off into the sunset that is our honeymoon while we feel so good we can't come down from our high until our twenty-fifth anniversary."

"Why stop there? Let's go for fifty!"

"I'll be in my nineties by then!"

"So? Doesn't mean we won't still be kicking some ass around this town!"

They gazed into each other's eyes, on the verge of leaning in for a kiss. Brandy didn't care that her fiancée's lips smelled terrible, or that kissing Sunny in her current, inebriated state might be technically illegal. Yet she would take those hands, nuzzle her nose against Sunny's, and think of more words to say.

Too bad she took too long.

"Goes to show that everyone settles, I guess." Two women stepped out of the bar, one lighting up a cigarette the moment the door closed behind her. The other woman grabbed onto the handrail before she splat her face onto the parking lot. "Some people give up good sex, others give up their everyday sanity…"

The other woman laughed so loudly that she had to be drunk. "If you're Sunny Croker, you give up both, apparently!"

"Are you surprised? Dr. Meyer has always come across as a stuck-up bitch. I'm glad I started seeing that other doctor, even if she's half an hour away. It means I don't have to put up with being told my diet sucks. Like, I know that! Who cares? Besides, do I want to discuss my sexual health with someone whose idea of a good time is being a pillow princess? Like, there are hot pillow princesses who make you want to work for it, and then there's Dr. Meyer, who..."

They both paused. Blood began to boil in Brandy's ringing ears.

"Wet fish!" both women exclaimed at once. They doubled-over in laughter, feet scrambling down the steps while cigarette smoke danced in the late spring night.

Brandy stood back from Sunny, who hung her head and grumbled something her fiancée couldn't hear.

"What were those women saying about..." Brandelyn didn't have to ask. She had two perfectly working ears. Those words were in English. From the way Sunny blushed and looked as if she would rather be anywhere than here, she knew something about this. "Why are they commenting on *our* sex life?"

"It's my bachelorette party," Sunny explained a little too quickly. "People make up shit because they're jealous."

Brandelyn opened her mouth to demand something. Yet the bar door slammed open, revealing Anita as she reached for Sunny. The implication that it was time to *go* was raw.

"The natives are growing restless in here," Anita said with *way* too big of a grin. "It's time for the big girl to make her reappearance for the rest of her presents and some games. Maybe it's time for you to go, Brandy. Assuming you've said everything that…"

Brandy rounded on Anita. "Why are people commenting about our sex life?"

Anita snapped back like she had been slapped in the face. Oh, that wasn't shock. That was "*oh shit!*" Caught!

"I may have said something really, really stupid," Sunny fessed up. "I'm sorry, Bran."

"Did this something have to do with me being a *wet fish?*"

"Ah, well..."

Anita not-so-subtly motioned for Sunny to get back in the bar. A small group of women, most of whom Brandelyn barely recognized when her eyes glazed over in the red of anger, pushed by with unsolicited judgments on their lips.

"Better get back in there, Sunny!" one of them shouted. "Someone started taking off her clothes! It might be your last chance to see a pair that's not telling you what to do!"

Everyone turned around to laugh. Unfortunately for them, that meant they saw Brandelyn glaring at them from the darkness.

"Oh, shit!" From the way those tipsy women scattered, they must have been Brandy's patients. That was the extra kick to the teeth – knowing she would be seeing them soon, and they would *definitely* remember her.

"Somebody gets a little mouthy when she's drunk, huh?" That was directed at Sunny, who scuffed her shoes against the concrete and looked like she was about to vomit her liquid dinner. "Well, sorry I crashed the party."

Brandelyn collected her bearings – what were left of them, anyway – and kept her head up as she turned to the ramp. "I'll leave you be."

"Brandy, wait…" Sunny grabbed the railing, but didn't make it much farther than the first part of the slope. "I'm sorry! I didn't mean…"

Brandelyn didn't stop to hear apologies. She kept walking, ignoring the cajoles of drunken women who apparently now knew quite a *bit* about her personal life, as filtered through a jilted, drunken woman at her bachelorette party. It was one thing for a woman like Anita to hear a few unsavory things in private confidence. Quite another for half of Paradise Valley's gossip mongers to pick up the half-truths and spread them around like summer wildfire.

She made it all the way to her car, where she sat down, plopped her purse into the passenger seat, and banged her forehead against the steering wheel. Her first, loudest sob drowned out the monotonous honking that raised the ire of more than one person in the street.

Brandy had half a mind to run them over.

Chapter 14

SUNNY

"I can't believe I said that." Sunny held back another noxious burp that carried with it the remnants of her drunken mistakes. The sun was so bright that she swore her brain was about to explode and dribble out her ears. Every time she opened her eyes, she saw the searing sight of Brandelyn, her ire as powerful as the blazing sunlight threatening to pull Sunny's ocular orbs out of her head. *Look at me, super hungover and still remembering words like "ocular."* It was instinct. Pure, literary instinct. She couldn't tell a soul what the hell "ocular" *meant,* but by God, she remembered that was the word to use.

Anita wasn't hungover, but she might as well have been from how she looked. Perhaps that was pity swarming her face. The same kind of pity she offered students when they failed yet another English test. *"I know you try your hardest, Sunny,"* Ms. Tichenor would say to her biggest flop of a student, *"but I can't help you if you reach this point and still don't know the difference between 'you' and 'you're."*

"I'm still reeling from the secondhand embarrassment you passed out like booby candy last night." Anita shook her head. "When you decided to have that sixth beer, I knew things were going to get bad."

"You could've stopped that sixth beer, you know," Sunny spat. "Told you to get a Coke."

"I *did* get you a Coke! You were the one who dragged your own ass up to the bar and got 'one more beer, because my fiancée looked at me like I'm Charles Manson.'"

"I did not say that."

"You totally did, and it *almost* worked getting people to stop parroting that 'wet fish'. Seriously, you had to go with fish? *Wet* fish?"

"I'm *sorry*."

"Don't apologize to me. You should be apologizing to Brandy. Now everyone in town thinks she's terrible in bed and will tease you two relentlessly about it for the next twenty years. Rumors like those do *not* die down, especially when it helps every mediocre woman around feel better about their own lackluster love lives."

Sunny snorted. *Ow. That hurts my head.* "You would know something about that, huh?"

"You're talking to the woman who got caught fingering her girlfriend at the drive-in. Remember the drive-in? Remember *that?*"

"Don't deflect. I remember drive-ins *and* everyone twiddling their fingers at you every time you entered a room."

"For the record, we only got caught because Bonnie has a very intense O face."

That was the last thing Sunny wanted to think about as she stewed in how badly she messed up the night before. *Brandy must be so embarrassed. She won't talk to me.* To think, Brandelyn had come all that way to personally apologize and make a few of Sunny's dreams come true. That was how she was repaid? With rumors about *her* O face spread around town?" *It's all my fault. What kind of monster am I?*

A veritable monster.

Sunny was on the verge of tears as she faced reality. Brandy was out there somewhere, right now, shrugging off the hell her fiancée had shoved into her face. *She had come to apologize to me. Her! Apologizing! To me!* While it wasn't beyond the realm of possibilities, Brandelyn was a proud woman who didn't like to admit she was wrong. Everyone had their faults, of course. So happened Sunny was willing to overlook that personal fault because the good things about Brandy made up for that. *She overcame that flaw for two seconds to actually apologize, and that's how I respond?*

In the drunken heat of the moment, Sunny had lashed out the only way she knew how. Sober sunny, however, looked in the mirror and decided she didn't like what she saw. Or what she saw beyond her own reflection.

Brandy wasn't simply somewhere stewing in her embarrassment. She was hurt. The thought that *Sunny* was the one to hurt her only made it worse. It wasn't supposed to be like her. Her! Sunny Croker! The woman everyone said was as bright as her name and the friendliest gal around town. (When she bothered to go into town, anyway.) When Brandelyn and Sunny announced their engagement, it was to sage comments about how compatible they were. Two sides of the same coin. Opposites attracting, instead of reacting. Sunny would help mellow Brandelyn out, and Brandy would bring Sunny out of her shell. Instead, the stress of the wedding had completely thrown them out of whack. Brandy was so *un*mellow that the whole town felt those powerful reverberations, and Sunny had become more of a shadow than a ray of light.

Brandy was right. This wedding would simply be one forgettable day in most people's lives. The marriage itself was more important than a *wedding*. The wedding was simply a means to an end! Who cared if they got married in the woods or in a church? On the beach or in city hall? All that mattered was making the commitment to build a home together and bringing out the best in each other.

The offered olive branch was inadvertently snapped in half, and Sunny had no one but herself to blame. It was up to her to somehow make it right. Immediately. Because the wedding was in a few days, and she would be *damned* if she was the reason it went up in flames.

"Hand me my phone," she said, renewed purpose crowning her voice. "I've got a call to make."

Anita stared down the look in Sunny's eyes. Only when she received confirmation that Sunny wasn't going to call Brandy – and make things worse, of course – did she slide the phone over and fold her hands upon the table.

There was one emergency contact in Sunny's phone that she was about to call for the first time ever. A contact that had been placed there in case something unfortunate ever happened to Brandelyn... and her mother had to know.

Hildred Billings

Chapter 15

BRANDELYN

"Would you turn that frown upside down?" Cathy scoffed in her daughter's direction. "It's your bachelorette party. You're not *allowed* to frown."

Brandy supposed one could call this a bachelorette party, although it looked nothing like Sunny's drunken revelry at the local watering hole. There were no uninvited guests joining in and throwing breast-shaped erasers at the stage. No tacky, colorful drinks with naked lady straws. No hooting, no hollering, and definitely no *drunks*.

Just how Brandy supposedly liked it.

Her mother and sister surprised her with a trip to the coast, where they had the balcony of an upscale lunch spot to themselves. Freshly caught seafood sizzled on grills, spritzed with lemons and garnished with fresh herbs. Home fries cooked to perfection accompanied seasonal fruits. Every glass was filled with a respectable cocktail, although Cathy was already on her second mimosa. So was Brandelyn, though. The more she thought about her wedding, the more likely she was to indulge in a little champagne.

She hadn't spoken to Sunny in three days. Well, nothing more than a few short, snippy sentences. The wedding was still on, supposedly, but the rift between them only continued to grow. Brandelyn had been scandalized by the gossip around town. While nobody said it was about *her*, specifically, she knew the truth. The "wet fish" on everyone's lips was Brandelyn Meyer, the woman who was scheduled to have the wedding of the year in Paradise Valley. Oh, but one shouldn't expect too much from the wedding night. Poor Sunny!

She would be doing all of the work! Good thing Brandelyn was nice to look at, huh? Because that's all Sunny got.

Her mother assured her it would pass. Honestly, Cathy was much more lackadaisical about the affair than Brandy anticipated. *I was so embarrassed to tell her why I was upset with Sunny.* Cathy had raised a minor stink when her daughter came home Saturday night on the verge of tears. Hadn't she gone out there to apologize to Sunny? Why was she crying like she had been stood up at prom? Gosh, did she have to make *everything* about her?

Not until Brandelyn gathered the courage to confess did her mother understand. To a point. "*All right, it's been two days. Go talk to her. I plan on attending a real wedding next weekend. Make it happen!*" Yet Brandelyn didn't have the heart to return Sunny's calls, much like Sunny hadn't returned her calls. *Now I know how it feels. Guess we can all go home now.*

She had been looking forward to her bachelorette party surprise ever since her family arrived from New York. Her mother claimed to have looked online for "the best spot for what I have in mind," which naturally translated to *"I really want to go to the coast, so we're going to the coast."* Brandelyn loved the idea, though. Just her, family, and a few close friends who could make it? It should've been paradise. The day was clear and warm. The ocean was calm at that time of day. The few people on the beach behind them kept to themselves, with only a few dog barks to take them out of the moment.

Yet Brandelyn could hardly look some of her friends in the eye. Mayor Karen Rath did everything in her power to avoid talking about what happened at Sunny's bachelorette party. Oh, no, she hadn't been there, of course, but she heard all about it Monday morning when she came into her office at city hall. When she saw Brandelyn that day, she offered a demure smile and said, "I'm sure everything will blow over soon."

The party was more akin to a wedding shower than a bachelorette party, but with the focus on Brandelyn, she could pretend that Sunny had no part in it. Even when she unwrapped the new place settings she had been asking for ever since she last perused a Macy's. The bright yellow and green Fiestaware sets would look adorable in Sunny's cottage, a place Brandelyn had been considering spending more time during the beautiful summer months. *That's how it should be. I'll stay there during the summer, she'll stay with me during the winter... we were going to figure it out, eventually.* Sunny had conceded to change her address to Brandelyn's house because it was bigger and more practical. (Although she would now have to pay city taxes, since at the moment she lived outside of Paradise Valley's limits.) Except what would Brandy do in return?

She loved that little cottage. It was where they first made love... and where they last made love. *Was that what she was thinking about when she made those horrible comments at her party?* Brandelyn hid her sniffing behind the box of bright green Fiestaware. Everyone who noticed politely looked away.

"I just... really love it, Mom. Thank you."

"Aww." Cathy held her hand to her chest. "Look at my little girl. Making a home for herself and her future family." That kind smile soon turned into a frown at her *other* daughter.

"Yes, yes, Ma!" Lizzie tossed her napkin down onto her empty plate. "City hall! Shotgun wedding! I know!"

"Well, I know a thing or two about that myself," Karen said, because she always loved to overshare about her marriage when she had a mimosa in her. *That's all right. She bought Sunny and me a spa day here on the coast.* "Wasn't city hall, but let me tell you, my mother gave me some dire looks when my ex-husband and I had to have a flash wedding at the American Legion Hall. Ah, well. My son is in college now! So, it wasn't all bad."

"Your daughter is an honor student at the high school, yes?" Brandelyn welcomed the change in topic that took the focus off her. "Was Anita Tichenor one of her teachers?"

Karen instantly realized where Brandy was going with this. That was the only explanation for the fake smile through gritted teeth and an extra clench to her mimosa. "Yes. English. Christina really loves her."

Of course. Everyone loves Sunny and her best friend. Brandelyn didn't hold anything against Anita, who had done her best to damage control an unfortunate situation. Yet anyone who was a best friend of Sunny's right now wasn't necessarily on Brandy's side. *I can't believe there are sides right now... what are we doing?*

"Brandy, hon." Cathy moved aside the gift bags. Some colored tissues attempted to fly away in the sea breeze, but Cathy stuffed them down beneath boxes of Fiestaware and the brand-new cappuccino maker. "There's one last little present we have for you before dessert." She cleared her throat. "It's a bachelorette party, after all."

Half the smiles at the table disappeared. "Uh..." Brandelyn said. "Don't tell me you hired a stripper." Cathy? Hiring *strippers?* Even for her lesbian daughter, that was impossible. Brandy would only believe it when she saw it.

"A *stripper?*" Cathy overcompensated her awkward laughter. Was it supposed to assuage Brandelyn's fears that her mother had personally hired sex workers to descend upon this humble bachelorette party? Because it's wasn't working. It was only making everyone in the room look at her as if she really had hired strippers.

Lots and lots of strippers, based upon that laughter.

"You're hilarious, dear." Cathy finished her second mimosa and smacked her lips in glee. "Ooooh, a stripper! We couldn't make your sister *that* jealous that you're getting so much special treatment."

"Mom!" Lizzie snapped.

Cathy ignored her. "You have a special present in the private dining room. Go on. Ask the hostess up front about it... oh, there she is!"

The woman in jeans and a black blouse approached Brandy with a blindfold in her hands. "No," she whispered to the bride. "It's not a stripper. We wouldn't allow that on these premises."

Brandelyn wasn't sure how relieved she was. *Not at all, really.* That only meant something crazier was afoot. If she couldn't anticipate her own mother's actions? She might as well throw herself off the patio and land face first in the salty sands of Oregon's coast.

"If you have to be blindfolded," Monica said, while perusing Instagram on her phone, "then it's naughty, whatever it is!"

"It's not naughty!" Cathy insisted. "What kind of pervert do you all think I am? Look at this lunch. Isn't it classy?"

"Tell you what." Brandelyn stood, accepting the blindfold from the hostess's hand. "I'll put this thing on if you get my mother another mimosa. She's not driving, anyway."

Brandy couldn't tell who hooted and who cheered her on to go "get that surprise you deserve." She was too busy being blinded to the world. *I have to admit, this is a little exciting...* Everyone insisted it wasn't a stripper, but for it to be for *her* implied it was more than a little special. Besides, if it *were* a stripper, odds were good her mother got her a male one, because

Heaven forbid she and Brandy stay on the same page of these things.

The hostess tested the knot Brandelyn tied behind her head. *I can still see a few things... plenty of light around here.* That would change as soon as she was led inside, where a few of the other diners choked on their food and drink to see a woman wearing a T-shirt that said BRIDE walking blindfolded into another room.

"Have a seat right here, Miss." The hostess guided Brandelyn to a chair by a window. She felt the draft and heard the ocean waves on the other side of the glass. Perfect combination to enjoy the afternoon by herself. If that's what she were there to do, anyway. This was a blindfolded woman, after all. "Enjoy your party."

She was gone within a minute. Brandy pressed her hand against the window and sighed. *Maybe my gift is getting some peace and quiet.* Yet too much peace meant thinking about her predicament with sunny. Not really much of a gift, now was it?

Someone placed a hand on her shoulder.

Brandelyn almost knocked her whole body against the window. The gasp of fright overcoming her was only mitigated by the familiar scent of a woman she knew better than she knew herself.

"Huh?" Brandy ripped her blindfold off, as if that had been part of the plan all along. Before her stood Sunny, wearing nothing slinkier than a pair of denim shorts and a peachy tank top that showed off her gardeners' biceps. Yet it was the apologetic look on her face, tipped with pink lips and a pair of tender brown eyes, that almost made Brandy come undone. "Sunny? What are you doing here? Are you my surprise?" Brandy thought about it for two more seconds. "Wait. What did my mother have to do with this?"

Sunny held up her hands to get Brandy to stop talking. "I called your mother on Sunday. Told her that I really need to make up what happened to you in some way. She told me that your bachelorette party was happening today and that I might come by to say hello... like you came by mine to say hello."

Don't I seriously regret it, too. Brandelyn could be living in blissful ignorance right now as she prepared to marry the supposed love of her life. "Everyone in town is talking about me like I'm some..." She bit back the rest of her words. She couldn't bear to repeat what she had heard.

"I know. I'm sorry." Sunny clutched her hands before her, as if she were about to get down on her knees and beg for forgiveness. She didn't. Her fists merely pressed against her chest, facing the fact that she would not yet get to touch Brandelyn. "I also know that me saying I'm sorry doesn't change the fact that I made a real mess of things."

"Why would you ever *say* something like that if you didn't think it was true?"

Sunny looked up from the floor, her big, bright eyes so clear that Brandy nearly gasped. *I don't care how beautiful she looks right now. She should be ugly crying and groveling on the floor!* Oh, she thought that, yet the truth that Brandelyn could look into those glistening brown eyes for the rest of her life. Wasn't that one of the many reasons she wanted to marry this woman?

"I don't think it's true. You're a great lover, Bran. I wouldn't be fooling around with you after all this time if it weren't true!"

"But you said those things... and it's not like we really do it much anymore..." Brandelyn chomped down on her bottom lip before it began to wibble. "I know we don't have to make a lot of love for us to have a great relationship, but when you tell the whole town I'm like a wet fish, I can't help but think it's true!"

"You know why I said that?" Sunny lowered her hands, palms open and fingers spread. "Because I thought of the meanest thing I could say when I was drunk. I was still raw from how I felt after our last fallout. Then Anita dragged me into the bathroom to knock some sense into me, and then you showed up, and..." She sighed. "I'm sorry. That's all I can say. I can't take it back, I can't change what people are doing and saying... but I can apologize. I can tell you that I'm deeply sorry for what I said. And that I love you, Bran."

Brandelyn had been prepared to rip a new asshole into her fiancée's tush. Honestly, she should have! Sunny was right. She couldn't change what she had done or what effect it had on the town. Brandy didn't care if it would blow over within a couple of weeks and everyone moved on to some new scandal. It still hurt, like a weight pulling down her heart through her ribcage.

"You want to marry me after all that?" Brandy asked. "Do you still want to marry me after I've made you wear clothes you don't want and completely took over all the planning? You still want to be with me although I'm not any good in bed?"

"Brandy!" Sunny was supposed to be a special gift. Yet her presence only ripped a hole open between them, one bigger and more menacing than before. *Why does it have to hurt so much to look at my own fiancée?* Sunny didn't get rumors about her. Nobody looked at her and thought she was totally a control-freak who made a great doctor but a terrible girlfriend. *Everyone* loved Sunny! They wouldn't believe a rumor like that about her for a single second, but about Brandy?

This only exposed a truth about herself that Brandelyn never wanted to address. It didn't matter if her prowess in bed was something anyone considered a problem. All that mattered was that her personality was so reprehensible that nobody paused to think about the veracity of certain rumors.

They simply expected it. Because they wanted to.

"Of course I want to marry you." Sunny stepped forward and took her fiancée's hands. "All I've been able to think about ever since you proposed is how much I love you! Sure, this whole wedding thing has us jacked up, but it's gonna be over soon! I'll wear whatever you want me to wear, Bran. I'll haul my ass into the cutest church in town if it means you'll have the wedding of your dreams. I *want* your dreams to come true! That's what I signed up for when I said I loved you!"

Brandelyn was soon swept into an embrace that knocked a single sob out of her. After only a moment's hesitation, she wrapped her arms around Sunny and reveled in the familiar feeling of the woman who was meant to be her night and day. *She's my sunshine after the sun goes down. That's what makes her so Sunny.*

"I love you," Sunny repeated, voice cracking. "I only want to be married already. Let's put all of this behind us and move forward with our lives. Together."

Brandelyn hugged her tighter. Pressing her body against Sunny's had never felt so good.

Or relieving, for that matter. Almost as if everything she needed and wanted was right here, ready to be hers, forever.

Chapter 16

SUNNY

The day of her wedding arrived, yet Sunny still wasn't convinced she was getting married.

She sat in her underwear – the department store lingerie she purchased for this occasion, no less – at the foot of her bed, gazing into the nothingness that was her bedroom. *I wish I could say that it's cold feet preventing me from getting dressed.* If anything, her feet were sweaty. The carpet held in the heat of the warm summer morning. A gentle breeze occasionally blew by, and the birds in the trees outside her cottage window chirped as if they had a great conference to conduct. The shouts and responses of Debbie the wedding planner and a few of her hired hands put the finishing touches on everything outside. In two hours, Sunny would be getting married.

Brandelyn had been awaiting her at rehearsal the evening before, and the smiles they gave one another reassured everyone in their party that they had peacefully made up and intended to go through with the event. Yet their practice kiss had been hollow. Nerves bubbled up Sunny's throat as if she were ready to throw up at any moment. The knot in her stomach had her pressing her hand against it every three seconds, wondering if her period would make an obnoxious appearance a few days early. Brandelyn may have planned their big day down to the perfect moment of her cycle, but Sunny would be lucky to make it through most of the honeymoon without Aunt Flo deciding to tag along.

It's the perfect day for getting married. The sun was bright and warm. The air was full of the scents of freshly cut grass and flowers. Laughter carried on the wind, for even Debbie and her crew were nothing but happy smiles as they prepared for the biggest lesbian wedding of their summer. Sunny's family were still cleaning up the big breakfast they cooked in Waterlily House, not that the bride had any appetite. Her mother and Aunt Jill joked that she was nervous about saying the vows and having her first dance as a married woman. Sunny was more concerned that she was making a big, *huge* mistake.

So... cold feet.

She couldn't pinpoint where this came from or how normal it was. Regardless of the fights she and Brandelyn had recently, would she have felt the same way? Was Sunny Croker destined to hyperventilate a little on the morning of her wedding? Wearing nothing but her underwear, no less?

Her hands disappeared between her thighs. As her knees closed in on her forearms, Sunny hunched over and let out a breath.

It did not help her feel better.

"So, what's it gonna be?" Dressed in nothing but a white slip that showed off more than what was publicly kosher, Anita entered the bedroom with her bridesmaid's dress slung over her shoulder. The bright pink fabric poked out of the bottom. *She's gonna look so good today.* After receiving the *exact* shade of pink Brandelyn demanded, Anita went out and bought a white cocktail dress that flattered her figure and showed off her long, modelesque legs. *"I don't get to wear something like this to work!"* she had said when she first showed it off to Sunny. When it came back from its dye-job, the rosy pink only brought out more of Anita's color and flirtatious personality as she pranced about Sunny's cottage. *I'm cool with that.* Sunny wouldn't mind her bridesmaid deflecting the attention off the bride. Well, *that* bride, anyway.

"Huh?" Sunny asked, morose.

"Will you be the dashing groom in a suit?" Anita pulled open the closet doors to reveal the finely pressed suit Sunny had brought back from the city a few days ago. "Or will you be the beautiful, blushing bride in her humble dress?" Fingers flitted over the dress, still put away in its bag. "Hurry, now, the bonus round is about to end!"

"Don't do that." Sunny slumped onto her side. "No matter which I choose, I feel like I picked the wrong one. Oh, and I've wasted money either way."

"Come on. You can wear this fancy tux to other functions in the future. Can't exactly wear a dress to…"

"The tux is a rental," Sunny reminded her friend. "I won't be wearing it anywhere else." She had plenty of nice dress clothes for formal events, anyway.

"So…" Anita closed the door on the tux. "You know the answer, then."

Sunny curled up into a helpless ball. "Am I doing the right thing by marrying Brandelyn?"

While Anita did her best to hide the massive eyeroll gaining traction in the center of her face, Sunny still saw it. Coming for her, no less. "Don't do this to me, Sun. I'm your friend, not your fall girl for when you jump into your car and drive all the way to Ashland to start your new life in a lesbian commune. Also, I'm not following you if you become a runaway bride. Although Brandy might. I bet she'll drag her big dress into the nearest truck and run you down somewhere on I5."

Sunny snorted in mild amusement. The image of Brandy in a giant bridal gown – the kind to swallow her whole, of course – brought with it the few moments of mirth Sunny had been missing on her wedding day. "You know what I mean."

"Do I?" Anita asked. "Because nobody was more excited than you when Brandelyn asked you to marry her. Remember? You drove to my house and got out of your car screaming so loudly that I thought you had lost one of your limbs. Bonnie still has night terrors from it." She sat on the edge of Sunny's bed, but didn't try to touch her. "I thought you two made up after last weekend?"

"We did, but..."

"Don't tell me this is *general* cold feet. I can't do jack about that."

"All I'm saying is that I'm not 100% sure that Brandy is the woman I'm meant to be with for the rest of my life. This wedding has taken a toll on our relationship. What if it never recovers after today? What if I spend the rest of my life making concessions to keep her happy?"

Anita flung herself back onto the bed, the whole thing shaking enough that Sunny almost rolled onto the floor. "What if, what if, what if! Do you know how many times a day I hear that phrase from my students? The little buggers love throwing it at me. *'What if I lose my file, Ms. Tichenor?' 'What if I regret going to U of O instead of OSU?' 'What if my dad decides to leave my mom?'* Like, give me a break. I'm not a seer. I can't look into the future and tell you whether or not you're making the right decision about a major life event. You either do it or you don't! But I'll tell you what I tell my students." Anita rolled over, finger pointing right in Sunny's face. "You have to ask if you would regret *not* doing something more than having done it. Is the one college really more appealing, or are you being indecisive? Would you be more upset if you broke up with Brandy than if you ended up going through a divorce later? I mean really, Sunny, what's the worst that happens?"

"Like you said, a really messy divorce..."

"What's the alternative? Not getting married? Splitting up? Wasting all the money you've spent on this wedding and nothing happens? Come on. Is that really what you want? Or do you want to marry the woman you love? If you could make it through this wedding planning, you can make it through *anything*. Probably."

Sunny sat up, her feet finally touching the ground again. "You're right. I have to decide what I would regret the most. Damn the consequences!"

"Not quite what I said..."

But Sunny was marching to her closet, doors flying open as her determination only grew.

Chapter 17

BRANDELYN

Brandy made the point to *not* eat breakfast on the morning of her wedding. She didn't want to risk the bloat in her perfectly fitted wedding dress. She also didn't want to risk throwing up from the nerves exploding from both within and from all around her.

That meant she was more than a little woozy as she stepped off the stool Apple the seamstress used for last-minute alterations to the hem of the dress.

"Oh, look at you!" Cathy flashed a camera in her daughter's face. Brandy swore she was about to be sick. Again. "My little girl on her wedding day! This dress is prettier than I remember! You look like an *angel*!"

"I do?" Brandy turned to the mirror. She had commandeered Aunt Jill's guest room in Waterlily House for her glow-up, since she would be damned if she sat in a car with this thing on. (Let alone before the ceremony and the appropriate number of pictures.) She wouldn't risk a single crease or stain until the cake was cut! "Thanks, Mom."

They shared a hug – that definitely stuck a crease in Brandy's dress – before she went to find her sister and cousin in their dresses. Lizzie was radiant in her pink chiffon gown that sported a big bow in the back and an acceptable neckline. Much better than the tawdry dress she originally wanted to wear before Brandelyn stepped in and told her to "class it up for the wedding!" More city hall shotgun wedding jokes were shared as everyone remembered the cleavage Lizzie sported at her own wedding. "*As if we didn't know how you got a bun in the oven to begin with...*" Cathy always loved to hoot.

Monica wasn't an official bridesmaid, to keep the numbers even, but she also wore a pink dress and pinned a red rose to her bodice. She was in charge of the boys, currently running amok up and down the stairs of Waterlily House, but Brandelyn was too excited about her big day to yell at them for shaking the photo prints on the wall.

The photographer arrived right on time for the family photos and the pre-ceremony shots of the bride. Brandelyn corralled her nerves as she sat in a windowsill, her veil, gown, and bouquet arranged in such a way that she would be captured in such a radiancy again. Her mother shed more than a few tears behind the cameraman as she took multiple photos from different angles. Every time the words *"Such an angel!"* were uttered, Brandelyn smiled a little wider. *That's right. I am an angel.* That meant this was Heaven!

All the beauty! All the potential!

All the attention!

Debbie popped into the guest room fifteen minutes before the start of the ceremony.

"Brandy!" she hissed, hand waving the bride over to the doorway. "We need to talk."

The color drained from Brandelyn's face. What had happened? Were the caterers stuck on the highway? Had the flowers blown away in a strong breeze? Was Mayor Rath too sick to perform the ceremony? *I swear to God, Karen, if you bail on me on my wedding day, I'm making you pay for SO many tests during your next checkup!*

"What is it?" Brandelyn braced against the doorframe.

"There's been a slight change to the ceremony."

"What!"

"Sunny insisted. She, uh..." Debbie pulled at her collar. "She asked me to not tell you what she had decided, but you're to go on at the usual time. Just... don't panic if things are a little different."

Brandy had half a mind to grab Debbie by the collar and shake her. "What!" she repeated.

"Everything is fine!" Debbie backed away before the bride choked her. "You go on in ten!"

That did *not* help Brandy, who took one step toward the wedding planner before her mother intervened.

"Do you know anything about this?" she asked Cathy.

"Not at all. I hope everything is all right. Why would she tell you something like that if it wasn't that dire?"

Don't panic, huh? Brandelyn had no idea how to take that. She was stuck following her usual schedule, only now with a new layer of dread settling in over her. *I swear to God, Sunny...* Last minute changes had to be run by her first!

Not that Brandy had much opportunity to think about them when everyone was ushering her out of the house and to the start of the ceremony. Guests, dressed in suits and lovely dresses, sat in the rows upon rows of chairs meant to accommodate up to three hundred people. Murmurs erupted around Brandelyn, who could hardly avoid attention before reaching the head of the aisle created on the sprawling lawns of Waterlily House.

She had already forgotten about supposed changes by the time the sun beat down upon her bare shoulders. This was it. It was happening. She was getting married, and soon everything she had spent her whole life dreaming about would come to fruition.

How was she supposed to hold back the wibbling lips and tears sure to ruin her mascara?

Whispers of her stunning beauty erupted into the air. The live pianist from the Baptist church switched from a classical number to "In the Air Tonight," one of Brandy's favorite songs.

Orchid petals were already strewn about the walkway. Lizzie looked over her shoulder with a reassuring smile before their father appeared to take Brandy's arm.

"Oh, my, look at my gorgeous princess." He beamed in pride, although his nervous sweats already permeated his face and suit. Brandelyn overlooked that to instead rake in the compliments. *T-minus ten until we walk down the aisle...* "I can't believe this is happening. My oldest girl is getting married."

"Come on, Daddy, don't make me cry." It was bad enough her stepfather leaped into the aisle to snap a few pictures on Cathy's behalf. They had to wait for Debbie to whisk him away before the pianist switched to the wedding march. Three hundred guests stood. Brandelyn put on a big grin as she kissed her father on the cheek and turned the corner to gasps of delight. "I've got time to cry later!"

Her smile fell off her face as soon as she looked down the aisle.

Karen stood there, ready to officiate the wedding. So did Lizzie and Anita, two bridesmaids in matching pink dresses.

Yet Sunny was nowhere to be seen.

"Uh..." Brandy almost missed her cue to begin her walk down the aisle. What was supposed to be a blessed moment of lifelong triumph was suddenly bogged down in *panic*. "Where's Sunny?" she asked through a gritted smile.

Her father hadn't heard her. He didn't seem to think anything was amiss as he took the lead. Brandelyn searched for Debbie's face in the crowd and sent her the most anxious expression she could muster. She received two thumbs up, as if that made everything better!

"What is going on?" Brandy hissed in Anita's direction as soon as she was up front. Karen avoided eye contact. Lizzie was only checked-in long enough for a photograph. Beyond that? Brandy was still on her own. "Where the hell is my fiancée?"

Anita, who was pink with pride, jerked her head toward the aisle. "Why don't you chill out a bit and go with the flow, huh?"

Brandelyn couldn't say she appreciated that sentiment. Yet what other choice did she have? As soon as her father went to sit down, she was alone with nothing but her bouquet and hubris. After exchanging a pathetic look with Karen, Brandy turned around in her designated spot and tried to keep smiling for the cameras.

The wedding march continued. Brandy squared her shoulders and faced the head of the aisle.

The murmurs were renewed as soon as Sunny appeared. Apparently, she had bucked their rehearsed movements in the name of stealing the spotlight to herself.

Not that Brandy could blame her. She had never seen such a beautiful bride before.

Sunny wore a simple sleeveless gown that boasted a plain, heart-shaped bodice and a skirt made of yards of tulle. Her short, feathery blond hair held no veil, but the sparkling barrettes she wore above her bangs drew Brandelyn's eye as if that had always been the plan. A small bouquet of pink and purple pansies was clutched in one of Sunny's hands as the other held her skirt high up enough for her to walk in white ballet flats.

Everyone ooh'd and awed. The photographer went nuts, taking pictures of both Sunny and the shocked expression on Brandelyn's frozen face.

The selfish side of her demanded to know why all of her plans had been so unceremoniously overthrown. She knew she had told Sunny she could wear her dress, but did that mean she got to walk second? That she stole Brandy's thunder as the consummate bride on her wedding day? *This* was what everyone would remember from the ceremony. Brandelyn was no longer Princess Diana.

Sunny was.

Yet the overwhelming feelings bubbling within Brandelyn told her selfish side to shut the hell up.

She's so beautiful... Perhaps everyone around her assumed that the tears welling within Brandy's eyes were because her attention had been stolen. In truth, she was overwhelmed by the radiant woman walking down the aisle as if she had been born to become a blushing bride. It was a side to her Brandelyn had never seen before. *Here I am, sharing it with three-hundred people.* She was sharing the happiest day of her life with three-hundred lucky people.

Mostly with Sunny, who reached the end of the aisle with a smile on her pink lips.

"Hey," she said, handing Anita her tiny bouquet and reaching to take Brandy's hands. "We look pretty good together up here, huh?"

Karen sighed in reverence while the pianist stopped playing and the guests sat down. The hush falling over the wedding ceremony would be the last time either of them beheld silence for the rest of the day.

It was the moment for Brandelyn to look back on the past forty-two years of life. Forty-two years of hoping, praying, and planning. Everything in her romantic heart had led up to this precious moment. The most important vision her subconscious insisted upon was mired in self-doubt and confusion as she looked upon the cute woman in a simple, cheap wedding dress. What was that feeling in Brandy's chest? Disbelief? Fear? Anxiety?

Perhaps the answer was more benign than that.

Maybe she simply couldn't handle how perfect this blessed moment was.

Hildred Billings is a Japanese and Religious Studies graduate who has spent her entire life knowing she would write for a living someday. She has lived in Japan a total of three times in three different locations, from the heights of the Japanese alps to the hectic Tokyo suburbs, with a life in Shikoku somewhere in there too. When she's not writing, however, she spends most of her time talking about Asian pop music, cats, and bad 80's fantasy movies with anyone who will listen...or not.

Her writing centers around themes of redemption, sexuality, and death, sometimes all at once. Although she enjoys writing in the genre of fantasy the most, she strives to show as much reality as possible through her characters and situations, since she's a furious realist herself.

Currently, Hildred lives in Oregon with her girlfriend, with dreams of maybe having a cat around someday.

Connect with Hildred on any of the following:

Website: http://www.hildred-billings.com
Twitter: http://twitter.com/hildred
Facebook: http://facebook.com/authorhildredbillings
Tumblr: http://tumblr.com/hildred

Made in the USA
Middletown, DE
21 July 2021

44594306R00139